A Quiet Town No More

An account of a reporter's experience
at the Battle of Gettysburg

D0888017

By

Kevin Drake and Lisa Shower

PRESS

O ne of the most gratifying aspects of the creation of this book is thanking all those who have helped me and inspired me in various ways. I would like to show my sincere appreciation to:

Wayne Motts, Tim Smith and the Staff of the Adams County Historical Society

Rev. Roy Frampton- President Gettysburg Licensed Battlefield Guide Association

Bernadette Loeffel-Atkins at Battlefields & Beyond Military History Book Shoppe

Erik Dorr-Curator of the Gettysburg Museum of History

Randy Drais for all his help

My mother Anastasia Drake for her love of Gettysburg

And my wife and best friend Pam Drake who always picks me up and never stops believing in me

Kevin

My participation in the creation of this book would not have been possible without the support and encouragement of so many people. But there are a few that deserve special mention.

To the Thursday night "regulars" at the Adams County Historical Society who have helped me hone my research skills. I look forward each week to our evenings together! A special thank you to Tim Smith, historian at the Adams County Historical Society for teaching me to set the bar high and accept nothing less than the best I can achieve.

To my late parents, Armond and Betty Malandra, who instilled in me at an early age, a love of history and books. They would be amazed at how far I have come.

And for all the patience, support and love given to me everyday, all my love to my husband Rick Shower.

Lisa

A percentage of the profits of this book will be donated to the Adams County Historical Society in Gettysburg, PA

Prelude

The countryside radiated with a sense of warmth, vitality and prosperity. It seemed very easy to put the thoughts of everyday worries aside riding through countryside like this, I thought. It is hard to believe that our country is torn apart by a civil war! Oh, I know it to be true given what I've seen in my travels, but this tranquil countryside belies the fact that brother is fighting brother in a struggle for men's ideas to take flight.

It is late-June in 1863 and this war has lasted more than two years already. My travels as a newspaperman take me to many parts of the Union (and some Confederate areas as well, if the truth be told!), but I have just finished an assignment and am hoping to include some time to visit my good friend Charles Tyson and his new bride Maria in Gettysburg, Pennsylvania before returning home to my own lovely wife. Charles and Maria were just married this past April, I am anxious to see how they have settled into their new home.

This visit isn't strictly a casual one. I am always looking for a story and this time is no exception. This part of the country is relatively untouched by the war, so it should be interesting to see how these folks feel about the hostilities. It is my suspicion that they hardly ever think about what is going on south of them and little wonder, as the war will not likely ever head north again. Last summer, General

Lee went the farthest north that he would ever be able to bring his troops. In the peaceful southern Maryland town of Sharpsburg, Lee and his Army of Northern Virginia met up with the Army of the Potomac. The newspaper headlines of September 1862 reported the dreadful, bloody news of what has now been named the Battle of Antietam. Now there are reports spreading throughout the countryside that J.E.B. Stuart and his cavalry are very close to South-Central Pennsylvania and they are on a scouting mission for the Confederate Army.

After this sojourn with the Tysons in Gettysburg, I plan to head straight for home. Too many months have passed since last I saw my wife Mary and it will be pleasant to not only spend some time at home, but also to enjoy the amenities a large city offers. My companion Chester will also enjoy a break from our travels. He is a faithful, dependable horse. Although I am only a few hundred miles from home, this rolling countryside makes it seem a world away.

Charles Tyson
Picture courtesy of the Adams County Historical Society

June 27, 1863

What a beautiful day for a ride into the town of Gettysburg. Let's see - I am looking for 216 Chambersburg Street and it appears I am riding along York Street. I can't wait to see my old friend Charles Tyson and his new bride Maria. I wanted to spend some time with them considering I could not attend their wedding in April. I am hoping Maria is not angry with me - as a reporter, I am always looking for a good story and I was sent to Washington to cover President Lincoln's speeches. Unfortunately, the story was very time consuming and caused me to miss the wedding. I explained to Charles that as a reporter duty calls at any time of day, seven days a week. In this time of war I have to be ready to break that big story that will give me an edge over other reporters and I am not afraid of putting myself in harms way to obtain it. Since I am a new husband I want to provide for my wife and the family we are planning.

Now that I am through patting myself on the back, I need to get back to business. That must be Charles' photography studio over here on my left on what I believe is York Street. Gettysburg appears to be a very quiet and beautiful town, no wonder Charles always talks about it. The time is 3:30 in the afternoon and the studio looks to be busy, I will visit him later so not to disturb his business.

Let me look at my notes. Charles told me to stay at the Eagle Hotel. He told me once I get to the town "diamond" or center of town with the flagpole, to continue straight on Chambersburg Street and I won't miss it. Oh, what a nice little street, row houses and businesses neatly line the street. Here it is, the Eagle Hotel and what a grand hotel it is. There seems to be a crowd here as well. I will check in a little later, but first I want to see what else this town has to offer.

I would not be surprised if I am to return soon to Gettysburg, as I am told Charles' brother Isaac is on the hook to be the next one of the Tysons who will tie the knot. Maybe I can bring my wife Mary for that, as I am sure she would enjoy the trip and I the company on that long ride.

Now let me search for a store to purchase some supplies. We reporters are spontaneous creatures and are always prepared, that is, except when it comes to me. Mary often tells me I would forget my head if it wasn't attached and she is right, for I forgot extra paper for writing needs. Oh boy, would Mary have a chuckle over that. I spotted an older gentleman to my front. "Excuse me sir, but is there a general store in town…sir…excuse me, hey!" He just proceeded to walk away. Maybe that old man has bad hearing because he was pretty old? I would hate to think he was ignoring me. Oh, what's this, Fahnestock Brothers, now that looks like a large store and should have what I need. "Okay Chester, that's a good horse, you stay here while I run inside and pick up some supplies; after that we will get you some hay and oats for your dinner." Now let's see, where is all the paper in the store, this can't be all they have. Here are the supplies I need, but for such a big store it is not stocked as well as one would expect. Maybe the prices are high? Why is the store so empty? I asked. The clerk answered,

"The Rebs cleaned us out; where have you been, mister?" The clerk looked at me as if I had too much to drink and continued to wait on other customers. Everyone does seem very nervous. I heard the Rebels were about these parts, but I have been traveling for the last two days and so I did not know they came through Gettysburg or even near it. I noticed I was getting some looks from the folks in the store. Maybe because I am a stranger, who knows? Exiting the store I said, "C'mon Chester, let's get you something to eat."

It was another real hot day and can you believe it was June 27th already? The days are really flying by. Maybe with luck General Hooker will send General Lee and his army back into Virginia and this war will be over; that is, of course, if General Grant does the same thing in Vicksburg. Anyway, I can't wait to catch up on old times with Charles and Maria but I will not let it get out of control, respecting the fact that they are Quakers who are sensitive to certain topics, so I will select my subjects carefully. My wife sometimes tells me my mouth runs faster than my common sense and sadly, she is correct.

It is 5:30 in the late afternoon and I stopped by to see Charles. It was really nice to see Charles and Maria and catch up on old times and about their wedding. Now what I need to do is find a stall for Chester. Charles filled me in on what happened with the Confederates coming through town, no wonder the store was empty. Charles also answered my question regarding the absence of horses in the streets. It looks like the Confederates took them as well as a lot of livestock that they purchased or should I say "stole" with that worthless Confederate money. Charles gave me directions to a nice livery stable for me to leave Chester. He knew the owner so I felt good about leaving Chester in his care. He is such a good horse and I could not bear to see him not having a comfortable night's sleep after our long journey to get to Gettysburg. Charles' directions were good but I seem to be lost; oh my, where is Carlisle Street? While I stopped and looked around for Carlisle Street, I observed a small child no older than four or five years old looking trance - like at Chester from the side of the road. "Hello there young lady, what is your name?" She whispered something but I could not hear her. Just then a woman I assumed was her mother yelled, "Mary, you get over here. What did I tell you about getting so close to the street?" The little girl backed up. Her mother said, " I am very sorry if she held you up, Sir." "Not at all, I am not in any rush, just visiting," I said. She gave me that strange nervous look I received at the store earlier. What is it about being a stranger in this town? This time I decided to explain, "I am here to see the Tysons, who are my friends;

I am a reporter from up North and unfortunately I am unfamiliar with the streets in your town." She introduced herself as Mrs. Sarah Broadhead and her daughter Mary. I looked down and told Mary what a beautiful name it was. Mary gave me a big smile. I also then looked at Mrs. Broadhead and told her that Mary was the name of my wife. I told Mrs. Broadhead that my wife will be worried sick about me when she hears of what has happened in Gettysburg recently. She told me she is worried about her husband Joseph; she hadn't heard a word from him since he was cutting down trees along the roads with others in town, trying to slow down the advancing Confederate Army. Little Mary told me she missed her daddy but Mrs. Broadhead assured her he would be home soon. She also told me General Early had been through town taking everything. She said that the Confederates were a group of ragged, dirty men shouting about town and the worst was what they did to the black citizens. I asked what happened to them, but feared the answer I would receive. "They lined up all the black citizens in town they could find on Chambersburg Street and marched them away, probably down South into slavery. The crying and moaning of these poor people broke our hearts. We had also heard the Rebs were on the move up North and that they were burning the towns as they left them. We saw the fires in Emmitsburg and started to panic, but it wasn't the Rebs at all, it was some person in town that started the fire. Those fires scared a lot of the black folks and they left town quicker than jackrabbits. I would run if I were them, as far away from those Rebs as I could. Those people were hard working good people and now they are headed God knows where," she said.

Sarah Broadhead pointed out Carlisle Street to me, which was right off the town "diamond" and directed me to the livery stable. After bedding Chester for the evening, I once again encountered Mrs. Broadhead and asked directions to 216 Chambersburg Street this time, the Tyson's home address. She told me to follow her since they are her neighbors and she was on her way home.

Out of the corner of my eye I noticed that same old man who wouldn't give me the time of day earlier, grinning at me from afar. I asked Mrs. Broadhead who he was. "Oh, that's old man Burns and he is a bit prickly to speak with." This old man presented me with a challenge and I love a challenge. I first thanked Mrs. Broadhead for the chat and help with the directions, then patted little Mary on the head and told her what a brave little girl she had been and told them what a pleasure it was to talk to them.

I decided to approach Mr. Burns to try to spark up a conversation – I smelled a story brewing. When I reached about ten feet from him he yelled out, "What's your business here, mister? Ya better git before ya find yourself locked up for trespassin' and if you are sellin' something, I am not buyin'!"

"Oh no, sir," I assured him, not wanting to anger the old man further, but sensed a story written all over the old man. I told him, "I am a newspaper reporter up North and I was sent down to Gettysburg to talk to ONLY THE MOST RESPECTED CITIZENS in town. This is why I am here; so I am hoping to have a talk with you for my newspaper, a very PRO Union newspaper." For a brief moment, I could see the wheels turning in the mind of this old man; I have to admit that I was a little nervous. Just then he perked up in his chair and told me to come over and have a seat. He now seemed a little more excited with me when I asked his name (which he spelled out) and asked of his experience when the Confederate Army came through town. "Well mister reporter," he said, "I'll tell ya something, if those dirty damn Rebs come back through these parts again, I'm not gonna sit here on my backside and do nothing! I fought with General Scott against the British and taught them a thing or two, and I'll teach those Rebs the same lesson! Write that down for your paper young fella, and tell them John Burns said it and I am the constable here in Gettysburg!" He added that the Reb army also locked him up when they came through town the other day for being unruly, but was released when they left town. "Well, I showed em," he said and added he locked up some of the Rebel stragglers when General Early and his army left town. "Now if those Rebs think they're gonna come into my town again, they got another thing comin' and I'll whip 'em just like the Redcoats at Lundy's Lane," he said, "My gun is inside and a waitin'!" I thought to myself that I couldn't imagine living in this town and crossing paths with this old man; he is downright scary, especially if you are on his bad side. We talked for about twenty minutes as I wrote as fast as I could, then he said, "All right young fella, that's it, I am getting hungry and my belly is not waitin' for nobody when it needs to be fed. Come back tomorrow and I'll tell ya more about the war and General Scott," and then he just went inside. I was sitting there a bit confused on how abruptly he ended our conversation. I yelled, "Thank you for your time Mr. Burns" through the door and heard him just yell back "Yep" with a mouthful of food.

Well, I better check into the Eagle Hotel; it is getting late and I am getting tired. As I entered the lobby and looked around, it appeared to be a fine establishment. It was located at the corner of Chambersburg and North Washington Streets. It was very neat inside but it appeared that some items in the lobby most likely left with the Rebels upon their departure. The clerk at the desk checked me in and was helpful in answering some basic questions I had about the town. He said it was a town of about 2,000 to 2,400 people and that everyone was on edge about the Rebels passing through town, he added and hoped they'd never return. They even made off with some of my chairs and tables in the lobby, as well as food and liquor from the bar. But he added that he had hid the "good stuff". Since I showed him my credentials earlier, he must have felt safe telling me this. I asked if the other hotels in town suffered the same fate. "Not the Globe Hotel I suspect!" he exclaimed. I later found out the Globe was noted for its Democratic meetings and the Eagle for Republican meetings held there. Just then, a small boy ran past me as fast as a field mouse and hid behind the front desk. "Charles, I told you to stay with your mother in your room! Sorry about that mister, that's my grandson Charles. He can't stay put for more than three seconds. He is a good little boy and you might hear him scampering about. You're in Room #9 and my name is Tate, John Tate and I own this hotel. I don't usually pitch in here at the desk but folks in these parts are a might scared as you can imagine and that includes some of my help who didn't show up today."

I entered my room to organize and catch up on all my notes, not forgetting I must return home with a story. It is too bad I was not here when the Confederates were; I could have gotten a few stories from them. I wouldn't be afraid to talk to them as some other reporters would – heck, how am I going to catch my big break without taking some risks? I would be nervous about my horse, though. I couldn't bear losing Chester; he's a strong horse and would have drawn attention. We have had him for about five years now and my wife would be devastated if something happened to him. Well no worry, the Rebels are gone and I doubt they are coming back this way again. I think General Lee has more important places to invade than Gettysburg for a second time, so the folks here can relax and get back to normal. As far as this reporter, it's time to get some much needed sleep.

Eagle Hotel on Chambersburg Street
Courtesy of the Adams County Historical Society

John Burns
Courtesy of the Gettysburg Museum of History

June 28, 1863

What a beautiful morning. Let's see it is 9:30...NINE THIRTY!!!! I can't believe I slept this long. My gosh, I can't believe I was that tired and have been missing so much valuable time walking and talking to the people around town. Later, as I was having breakfast the thought occurred to me – "What if the Confederate Army was to come back to Gettysburg? What if they captured me and God forbid, took Chester and myself prisoner down south? Who would take care of my wife back home?" My goodness...listen to me, here I am the reporter who would walk through fire for that front-page story. Now I am behaving like a scared schoolgirl...worrying about nothing as mother always said. The Confederates are long gone and would never go that far north to my home, so why worry. Before you know it I will be walking around town scared as a ghost if my mind would let me and I can assure anyone who reads this, there will be NO ghosts in Gettysburg!

I decided to go out and see what the town had to offer. The editor of my newspaper grew up around these parts of Pennsylvania and went to school here. He gave me a list of places to see, but that was thirty years ago and I doubt he had the Confederate Army on his heels when he was here, looking to take him prisoner to some awful place. There I go again acting like that frightened school girl I swore I would never become!

Since it was Sunday, I decided to visit the Holy Ghost and take in Sunday services. There is nothing better to soothe the nerves than going to church. As my mother always said, "Never miss Sunday service because you will never know when you will need the Good Lord to help you out." I never was all that faithful like mother but truer words were never spoken considering my situation. After the service concluded, the congregation assembled out front and were talking about what happened two days earlier with the Confederates coming through town. Each person couldn't wait to tell their story about how they endured such a frightening event. This made me more nervous than before. I had to break the grip of fear, so I blurted out, "President Lincoln and our brave boys in blue will stop those Rebs from coming back, and you can count on that!" For a second that seemed as long as an hour, everyone turned and looked in my direction and stared in silence. I had forgotten I was a stranger in town; it was like time stood still then a young girl yelled out, "Oh yeah, mister, then where was President Lincoln and our army two days ago if you're so smart?" The crowd burst out in laughter. I apologized to any I offended and explained that I was in town visiting friends. Then the strangest thing happened - a small boy started yelling at the top of his lungs, "Union soldiers are coming! Union soldiers are coming!" Everyone in the crowd looked at me and grinned the biggest smile. A very large, kindhearted woman gave me the biggest hug I have ever received and said, "Thank you young man, oh thank you," as if I had something to do with the Union cavalry arrival. What a laugh I had when she turned her back.

The whole town turned out to welcome our protectors and it seemed as if the town came alive again with all the smiles on their faces and a little giddy-up in their step. People were soon handing out bread and cakes to our Union heroes who came to town to teach those Confederates a thing or two. People with buckets of water were handing out dippers to our thirsty troops as they passed. Oh, what a sight! I think it was also good for our boys in blue to see the reaction of the people in town and the hospitality they displayed.

As I looked at the crowd and wrote as fast as I could about the event, my eye caught sight of a man who looked to be in his fifties staring into the sky. Odd I thought, with all that is going on in front of him, why look at the sky? Was he ill? I approached the man and asked if everything was all right. He looked at me with a smile and said in a soft voice, "Yes my friend, just observing the clouds." I thought to myself that it was bound to happen that I would bump into at least one odd character here in Gettysburg. After talking to him I realized how very wrong I was; his name was Dr. Michael Jacobs and he was a professor of mathematics and natural philosophy at Pennsylvania College. He was one of the most intelligent men I have ever met. He told me he makes daily weather observations and records them. He also taught me a thing or two about the topography of Gettysburg. This gentleman was truly brilliant, but I doubt anyone a hundred years from now could care less about the weather in late June and July of 1863, but who knows. I thanked him for the chat and continued down Washington Street.

Along the way I saw Mrs. Broadhead and little Mary walking towards me. I said, "Hello, Mrs. Broadhead and a good day to you Miss Mary." She looked at the crowd and said, "Isn't it wonderful that the army is here? God bless you boys!" she yelled. Little Mary seemed to be more interested in the horses than the soldiers. I asked if there was a quicker way back to the center of town and Mrs. Broadhead told me to cut across to Baltimore Street to avoid the crowds. I bid them both "Good day" and headed in that direction, when all of a sudden I yelled "Ouch" as something hit me in the back of the head. I turned to see two boys run off but the smallest boy stood frozen, looking at the ball that had just bounced off my head. I asked, "Is this yours?" "Yep," said the boy, who added, "I'm really sorry mister, we were just playing when your head got in the way." Massaging the lump on the back of my head I decided to ask him his name. I was a bit steamed, but seeing the fear in his eyes I knew he was scared I would tell his parents and it reminded me of myself at that age. Thinking back when I was very young in school, I liked this girl in class, just like most little boys I decided to throw an apple at her to get her attention and instead it hit Mrs.

Wilkins, the headmistress. I knew what it felt like to be this boy. In a calm voice I said, "It's all right boy, you seem to be sorry about what happened. I think I can let it go, but what is your name?" "Charles, sir, - Charles McCurdy," he gratefully responded. "I live over there. Thanks for not telling my folks - I am already in big trouble for getting mud all over the rugs and floor." I asked him if he saw the Union troops come into town. He answered, "Did I see them? Are you kidding me mister, I was yelling at the top of my lungs when I first saw them until Mister Burns told me to pipe down." "Oh, so that was you yelling when I came out of church," I said. "Yep" he answered. "I'm going back over there and see if they bring up those big guns." "Well, Mr. Charles McCurdy, it was nice to meet you!" "And it was nice meeting you, mister, thanks for not telling my folks," Charles said.

I continued to walk around town and talked to many people, all of who seemed much relieved at the arrival of our cavalry. I met a Mr. Rupp who owned a tannery; Reverend Sherfy who claimed he had the tastiest peaches in Adams County and many other locals whose names I don't remember, but all of who seemed very friendly. Well it is late, I guess I can sleep a little easier tonight. I am writing home to my wife, she must be very worried by now that I am close to the Army of Northern Virginia. I didn't see a post office in my wandering today. I was told a Mr. and Mrs. Buehler are in charge of it. I will look for it in the morning and will mail this letter to her then although I may make it back home before she gets it. But at least she will know I was thinking of her while I was away. Now to get some much needed sleep.

June 29, 1863

Well, it looks like another night with very little sleep. I am still thinking the Confederate Army might still return to Gettysburg. Looking outside, I can see that it is pouring rain so I had better stay put until it stops. I fear it is going to be humid after this rain ends and make for an uncomfortable day.

Now for a chance to catch up on the news, courtesy of the local newspapers. Let me see what is happening in the world - can you imagine the boys in my office joking with me about reading a competitor's newspaper although a small town newspaper doesn't really count as competition, especially seeing as I am so far from home. The name of this paper is ummm, let me see, "The Compiler" and it says the Rebels captured and burned the Rock Creek Bridge as well as seventeen railroad cars. They also burned an ironworks in nearby Caledonia on Friday. I thought to myself, "What kind of people would burn things that non-combatants use or need, such as bridges, ironworks and railroad cars?" They came to Gettysburg with their worthless money and basically stole from the citizens of this fine town. I just don't understand it. I remember spending time down south with my cousins and family. Those good times, having picnics and playing games were priceless. My relatives and their neighbors were as nice to me as anyone north or south. How is it that their army would cause such destruction and be so cruel? It is even more worrisome if they go farther north and invade my home and town. Well, that settles it; I will stay until Wednesday morning and then I am going home. That should give me enough material for a story and get me home in time before the Rebels reach it. It's funny, but I am always running around chasing a story and now it feels like that story is chasing me.

I decided to check on Chester; the livery stable where he was being kept is well recommended by my friend Charles and Mr. Tate, so I felt good about that. I entered the stable to see Chester eager to go for a ride, but first he had to finish his breakfast. "Are you all rested up Chester?" I asked as I patted his head. "You're a good horse, so eat up because we are getting out of here in a day or two." But for today, we will just go for a ride. I will come back after you finish eating.

Walking around, I decided to see what other people I might meet in town, but before I do anything I needed to purchase some more paper. I headed back to the Fahnestock Brothers store because I knew they had what I needed. "Hello there!" I greeted the clerk. "Hello mister. Back for more paper?" he asked. "I hear you are a reporter for a big newspaper up north, it wouldn't happen to be with that New York newspaper, would it?" he asked. "No," I replied, "not that big of a newspaper but maybe someday."

When the other people in the store heard that I was a reporter, they seemed a little more at ease. Word traveled fast among the customers. It is likely because of the rumor that spies are all over these parts and me being a stranger, well, that would raise an eyebrow or two! After mentioning where I was from and the name of my newspaper, more people approached me and asked for the latest news. I explained to them that we are all in the same situation regarding the Confederate movements in our fine state of Pennsylvania and that I know nothing more than they do. One young lady, a Miss Ginny Wade said the rumors change by the day and most of the time she pays them no mind. She approached the subject of Southern sympathizers in town and mentioned how her brother Sam was almost captured the other day when the Rebs came through town. She told me, "There would be people in town that would really have made me very angry and would be very sorry if our Sam had been taken from us."

A small crowd had gathered in the store upon hearing our conversation. Another lady, I believe her name was Sarah King, spoke up and said she had heard the local blacksmith Mr. Doersom had been robbed of money by his former apprentice who rode with the Confederates. "I guess other than taking horses, livestock and buying things with worthless Confederate money the town was rather lucky, it could have been worse," Mrs. King said. "My real regret was having to watch the poor black citizens who were gathered up and taken back down south. I only hope they make it back home here once these Confederates are defeated and the war ends," added Mrs. King.

Upon leaving the store I discovered more about the feeling the locals had concerning the Confederates and also some of the friction among the citizens themselves. On the positive side, I grabbed the last remaining writing paper I could get my hands on. It seems to be an ongoing joke with my wife because I am always forgetting or running out of writing paper. She often says if I were a fireman I would forget my hose and ladder. I am really starting to miss my wife Mary and I am sure she is quite worried about me, but as I always say, "The story comes first." Now, on one hand I hope the Confederates never come back - that's the schoolgirl in me - but the brave eager reporter in me wishes they would come back and give me the story of a lifetime. To think how disappointed I was that nothing would ever happen in Gettysburg again and I was only one day late in meeting those Rebs face to face! And hope to get a second chance in meeting them.

Well, I am going to see Charles later for dinner and it is past 5:00 in the evening already. Let me return from my walk up Baltimore Street to the center of town. Reviewing my notes as I walked, I heard a familiar voice yell out, "Mister, don't trip on Miss Penelope!" As I looked up I saw nobody in front of me. Just then I tripped over something and lost my balance, landing on my backside and papers flying everywhere. Many a passerby laughed at my misfortune; when a small boy stepped forward from the crowd and helped me retrieve my notes from the ground and said, "I warned you, mister." I looked up and saw it was my little friend Charles McCurdy the young lad who clunked me in the head earlier. Upon standing, it appeared someone had buried the breech of a cannon in the ground. Odd, I thought, why would someone do this? I then realized it was in front of the office of the Compiler. How ironic since it was the newspaper I had just read this morning. I made a hasty retreat from that spot and Charles accompanied me. "Hey mister, ya want me to walk in front so I can warn ya about tripping again?" he asked with a chuckle. "No, I think I can handle it Charles, but thank you for trying to warn me before I fell. That was nice of you." Then he replied, " I think we are even, mister, after I clunked you on your head with my ball." He started to laugh and that attracted attention. I asked why he was laughing and he said, "Now you got a lump on your backside to match the one on your head!" My desire to get away from the Penelope incident was quickly overshadowed by the laughter of the townspeople upon hearing little Charles. It was all in good fun and it was then that I realized that I was being accepted by these people and no longer a stranger. But I still wanted to know why Penelope was buried there.

Penelope the Cannon buried in sidewalk
Courtesy of the Adams County Historical Society

June 30, 1863

Finally, a restful night's sleep and what a beautiful morning it is. I think this will be my last full day in town and I will leave first thing tomorrow. As for today, I need to pick up some good gems for my story because my editor is expecting it. I can already envision what he is going to say; "The Confederates were in that town and you missed them? Did you go after them for the story? I would have." Sometimes he still thinks he is a twenty five year old reporter like he was fifty years ago.

I wish I knew where the cavalry went after they came through town Sunday; they just disappeared and have not returned since. I would feel a might safer knowing those fellows were here in town. It occurred to me that I needed to get the most recent newspaper that would tell me the latest movements of the armies. I decided to go into town and finish this story thinking that the sooner I was out of here, the better off I would be.

I greeted my faithful friend as I approached the livery stable, "Good morning old Chester; did you get a good nights sleep my friend? Let us get situated and tomorrow we are headed home." I adjusted his saddle and we rode out of the stall toward the Seminary. That might be a great view from that elevation of town, I thought. Just then I heard, "Good morning." "Oh, well, a good morning to you as well, Mrs. Broadhead," I responded. "This is my husband Joseph," she said as the man glanced at me. "Joseph, this is the man I mentioned who came to see old friends and write a story about our town for his newspaper." "Yes, I remember." Joseph exclaimed in a slight British accent. I dismounted my horse and shook Mr. Broadhead's hand, "What a wonderful family you have, sir; it is a pleasure to meet you." I said, "Likewise," replied Joseph Broadhead "I say, did you know the bloody Rebels captured me for a short while? I got away though." "Really" I asked, "how did you get away?" "I was exchanged for one of their men; it is lucky I was able to return home. The Rebs were good to me, but I am quite glad to be home" "As I am!" Sarah exclaimed as she gave her husband a hug while little Mary hugged her father's leg. "Well I would like to hear more, Mr. Broadhead when you have the time," I said. "How long will you be here?" Joseph asked. "Tomorrow or the next day, depending on how much material I collect for my story." "Okay mister, I will talk to you later; I am still quite tired and have a bit of catching up to do with my family," answered Mr. Broadhead. "Then good day to you all." I said as I headed to the Seminary to get that view of the town.

I didn't realize until I got up there how high an elevation it was, you can see the whole town from up there. It seems odd that no one is out along the streets this morning. To my surprise I can observe smoke from campfires in the western distance…Confederate camps I assume. With a feeling of impending trouble I noticed some riders headed my way. "What or who are they?" I asked myself out loud. "It looks like cavalry - but wait - three or four of them are wearing gray. Confederates! They are Confederates!" "I'll pretend I don't see them. C'Mon Chester; here is a nice field of grass to eat." I figured if I am seen letting my horse graze and avoid eye contact they will leave me alone assuming I am a civilian and not a soldier. I actually hoped they didn't spot me and they seem to be more interested in something in town anyway. They are pointing to the town and look somewhat agitated and confused. They then rode away very quickly, but why? What would have made them leave so quickly? Talking to myself again I muttered, "I'm not waiting around here any longer, this reporter is getting back to town and heading for home as quick as he can."

As I rode closer to town, I could hear cheering and singing in the streets. I wondered what was going on. Just then, about ten Union soldiers approached me about halfway up the road to the Seminary. "Hold up there mister," they said and then asked, "Who are you?" I told them my name but they glared at me and one of them in the back yelled "Check him, he could be a spy!" "A spy," I exclaimed, " I would sooner cut my own throat than turn against my country and the Stars and Stripes of the Union. Here sir,... here are my credentials." I handed him my press badge and papers. "Okay, sorry mister, but we can't take any chances; there are Confederate spies everywhere, you know," he replied. "Totally understandable, my good sir; glad to see you soldiers. I was just over by the Seminary when I spotted four Rebs on horseback." The Union cavalrymen all stared at me. "Rebs you say? You observed Rebs up there?" "Yes captain, right up there looking over the town just minutes ago, but they took off like a shot after spotting you." By the way captain, who is in command of you fellas?" I asked. "Why General Buford is, of course," the captain answered. "Is he going to be able to stop those Rebs? I would like to get home!" I exclaimed. "Ha ha!" Laughter rose from the group. "Are you kidding mister? General Buford is probably the best cavalry commander in this whole damn army, but you better forget about leaving town anytime soon. There are Rebel troops everywhere we are told. Let's go boys," the captain shouted!" as they rode quickly toward the Seminary.

As I rode into town, I could see Union cavalry coming up Washington Street from what I think is the Taneytown Road. I really hadn't learned the local roads well, but that was my observation. "Hurrah, hurrah for General Buford!" A cheer went up from the crowd. One soldier yelled back, "We have two brigades here to give the Rebels hell and send Lee back to Virginia." Another one yelled, "Seen any Rebs?" A young man answered, "Yes sir, out west past the Seminary." The people in town were overjoyed and so happy as if the biggest burden was removed from them and yet nobody knows just quite what is going to happen, I think everyone hopes they stay in town this time. I thought to myself that maybe by pushing Lee back toward Virginia, it would give me a chance to go home. Personally I think any fighting will be done toward either Cashtown or York; in which case I can slip out the back door so to speak, but I have to be certain. Well, one thing is for sure; the Rebs won't be coming back through Gettysburg with the Union cavalry here in town.

I heard some of the local girls singing to the soldiers the song "Union Forever" as people in town were handing out bread, cakes, water and anything available to help them and knowing it might and probably would be the last bite some of these soldiers will ever have if a battle should occur. One young woman to my left dropped an armful of food as she graciously tried to hand it out to our soldiers. I bent over and placed the dropped items back in her arms. "Oh, thank you sir, thank you very much," she cried. "It is my pleasure, young lady," I replied. "Oh, it is Miss Myers, I mean Salome Myers." "Here you go boys," as she continued to hand out bread. The soldiers took the food, yelled their thanks and trotted up Washington Street, including many who sang along with the crowd. A more cheerful sight I do not recall. I tried to write it all down as fast as I could. The soldiers, the excitement of Miss Myers handing out food and the added sense of security with the Union cavalry here in Gettysburg all added to the joy and excitement of the whole town. As the last of the cavalry moved up Washington Street, I decided to stop back at the Eagle Hotel. I was getting hungry myself and I also needed more paper. I thought how amazing it has been to witness so much thus far during my trip to Gettysburg and now knowing we were safe, I wanted more material for my story.

As I walked through the crowd I saw a sight that touched my heart. I saw a small child with very curly hair playing on the pavement in front of what I believed was her home.

Soldiers were in the streets and talking with some of the people in town. I then saw a soldier talking to a woman, whom I believed to be the mother of that cute little girl. The soldier knelt down and was talking to the child and she smiled at him and gave him a hug, and he kissed her on the cheek. As the man arose, I saw his eyes were welled up with tears. The soldier looked at the woman and said something about his young daughter back home as he pulled out of his pocket what looked like a scarf or large handkerchief with the face of George Washington and two flags of the red, white and blue imprinted on it. The little girl's face lit up with a big smile as the soldier handed it to her and told her, "This is the face of George Washington," and as he was giving it to her he added, "Say a prayer for our dear country, little girl and for me as well." Still wiping the tears from his eyes he turned to her mother and said, "Thank you ma'am." I believe the mother had tears in her eyes as well as she said, "Godspeed—and we will pray for your safety."

The mother turned to the child and said, "That was very nice of that soldier to give you that scarf, Emma, so please put it in a safe place in the house." That sweet little girl ran into the house with her new treasure.

I thought to myself how emotional it must have been for that soldier, perhaps a father with a young daughter back home who he feels he may never see again with the impending battle ahead. Then seeing this child that so reminded him of his own daughter back home, he gave her a kiss on the cheek and a present. This must have lifted his spirits as if his own child was there. And that young child who in the years ahead, will never forget that kind Union soldier who gave her a kiss on what could be the eve of battle and gave her a scarf to remember him by.

As I entered the hotel lobby and then my room, I saw one of the hotel clerks with my bags in his hands. "See here, those belong to me, how dare you enter my room and try to steal my bags?" I shouted. "But mister," answered the clerk, " I have been instructed to move you to another room, as this one is needed for someone else." "And who might that someone be," I bellowed, "if I may be so bold as to inquire?" I was hot...this business about moving me without my consent; who was this important someone I asked? It really steamed me and the clerk knew it.

"That would be me, mister," I heard from behind me. As I turned, I felt my fist clenching. How dare he, I thought, to take my room with no explanation or apologies. I turned completely around and discovered I was face to face with a Union officer, a general no less. I felt like my mouth had frozen, I could not speak. I just stood there like a fool hoping he wasn't going to give me a thrashing. "I need this room because of the view," he explained. "I am General John Buford and I'm sorry but that's the way it has to be. We've got a war going on outside and General Lee is just down the road a piece." I recovered my voice and humbly said, "Please General, please forgive me. Absolutely you can have this room with my compliments." As General Buford and his staff stood there I felt like a fool. These men came to help us and here I was giving them a hard time, how foolish I felt.

"General, can I do anything to help?" I asked. Buford looked at me, but it was as if he looked right through me, almost like he was watching the battle unfold on the wall behind me. He then told his staff, "I want no liquor sold or given out tonight. Write it and post it." "Yes sir," they said. I stood there like a third wheel...frozen. General Buford left the room and I followed him out of the Eagle Hotel thinking I might get some interesting material as well as satisfy a dying curiosity of knowing what else was going to happen next. Suddenly a hand was pushed into my chest. "That's far enough mister; the General's real busy right now," said one of Buford's staff officers. "And me thinks he would like his space," exclaimed a man in what I recognized as an Irish accent. "I'm sorry captain," I answered, "but I am a reporter." "Aye reporter boyo, 'dat wouldn't happen to be the New York paper, would it?" asked the captain "Oh no sir!" I exclaimed. "I am located here in Pennsylvania, just a small local paper." "Aye, if it's all da same, please let us do our duty dat we swore to the good Lord ta do!" the officer shouted. "May I ask your name, captain?" I asked. "Aye," he said, "I am Captain Myles Keogh and am one of General Buford's staff officers and I have to catch up to him." As he walked away I yelled, "General Buford can whip those Rebs, can't he or are you going to need infantry help?" Captain Keogh stopped dead in his tracks, turned around and walked towards me. Oh no, I thought, what have I done? What did I say? "Listen here Mr. Newspaper Reporter, I have fought in the ole country and parts of Italy and General Buford is a blessing to the people in the North. God never made a finer brigade general! Just because he is quiet doesn't mean he don't know what he is doing. Have faith in us and don't mention infantry to me again. Now off with ye boyo and report on something else and stay out of da way," he told me as he left the room. Even though it seemed I had riled him up some with my comments, he remained a gentleman in his scolding of me. I guess I had better learn military etiquette or I might never leave Gettysburg, hopefully I won't be strung up by our own troops for putting my foot in my mouth.

General John Buford
Library of Congress

I walked back into the Eagle Hotel to organize my things. I was confused. I had never been in a position that I didn't have an answer or a quick response to, but after what had just happened, I felt more humbled than a schoolboy forgetting to do his homework when called upon. It looks like I am learning things about myself as well. "Ahhh, get control of yourself, it is all in your imagination," I told myself. "Hey mister," I heard someone say and turned around answering, "Oh, yes Mr. Tate, what is it?" I said, "I would probably leave those soldier fellas alone if I were you," he whispered softly. "They have got important things to do." Mr. Tate instructed. Oh great, I thought to myself, now I have someone to reinforce all the dumb things I just did. "Yes sir, Mr. Tate, I don't want to be a pest to those soldiers, thank you and good day!"

I decided that I should probably stock up on supplies if I was going to leave town early Wednesday morning. I realized that it might take some shopping around as the town was still pretty wiped out of supplies. As I walked up the street I noticed a shop I hadn't noticed before. What's this? It looks like a confectioner's shop. Yes, they sell cakes and candies. Well nothing like a little penny candy to brighten your day, if there's anything left inside which there didn't appear to be. As I entered I greeted the owner with a "How do you do sir?" I gazed at a man no bigger then five feet tall with a very modest voice. He asked, "Can I help you?" I asked, "Yes, mister., um mister?" "Oh I'm sorry," he replied, "my name is Winters but the children call me Petey. I certainly don't mind as they are some of my best customers." "Oh I see," I said. "Well, I would like one of your ginger cakes and what are these?" I asked. "Oh, that's my specialty," Mr. Winters said, "molasses taffy sticks." "The children love them and I sell them for a penny." "Okay" I said, "let me have some of them as well." "The Rebs cleaned me out so everything is freshly made," Petey said.

Just then a boy about 15 years old walked in the shop. I remembered him being one of the boys that ran when I was clunked on the head by his little friend Charles. He entered the shop totally unaware of me standing there and said, "One molasses taffy stick, Petey" as he placed the penny on the counter. "Coming right up Albertus," Mister Winters replied. He then said to me, "This is one of our local young men, Albertus McCreary." As he looked up at me, I saw the expression on his face change. "Hello, Mister Albertus," I said. "We did not happen to meet the other day, did we?" I could see Albertus standing there scared to death. I flashed back in my mind to when I was 15 years old. Mother had made a delicious blueberry pie for the church picnic and she was letting it cool. I could not control myself. Oh, mother's pies were heaven on earth! I stuck my fingers in that pie and had a chunk of it. My mother asked, "Did you eat some of the pie?" already knowing the answer. I was thinking of a way out of this one and then realizing I had blueberry pie on my face, I was ashamed and I started to cry. "Oh, don't worry," my mother tenderly said, "we can put some fresh blueberries on top. No one will notice." Oh how I loved that woman! Now I was in the same position my mother had been in. "Mister Albertus, I have a ginger cake with nobody to eat it with, would you like some?" "Oh boy, you mean it?" Albertus asked. "I'm real sorry about the other day," he said. "If it doesn't spoil your dinner you may have some," I answered. Petey gave him some. "Thanks mister and thanks, Petey; I'll see you later," Albertus cried as he ran out of the store in a rush. "That was real nice of you mister," said Mr. Winters, "you can always see the good Lord in the innocent faces of our children." "Amen, Mr. Winters, amen," I answered adding, "This is the best ginger cake I have ever eaten" after eating a small piece. Mister Winters smiled as I left his store and said, "Thank you sir, please stop back again."

When I stepped outside I noticed that the sun was starting to set and decided to stop by the Tyson Photography Studio tomorrow to spend some time with Charles before I leave town. One thing about a small town is that everyone seems to know each other's business. I have met so many people. There was Mr. Solomon Powers, who told me about his lovely daughters and how proud he was of them. Can you imagine all those daughters? And according to their father, they are all very attractive. The young men in town must be very happy about that. I met Doctor Horner, Mr. Will and Mr. Forney. They were all very nice. And there was that young lady I met a few days ago tending to her sister after giving birth. Her name was…wait I know I wrote it down. Ah, yes here it is, Ginnie, G.I.N.N.I.E. McLean. No wait, her sisters name was McLean, Ginnie's name was Wade.

I saw my two little friends again and now with a third friend. Albertus, the boy in Winter's Candy Shop, little Charles and Gates Fahnestock, whose family I believe owns the family mercantile store. The boys told me they went into the camps of the Union cavalry and were given the duty of riding the horses to a stream for a drink. Imagine the excitement these boys will have telling their children and grandchildren about their contribution to the cause. As I walked to the Eagle Hotel to gather all my notes and retire for the evening, I decided to walk up Chambersburg Street toward the Seminary. I remembered the Confederate campfires that were spotted on the mountainside miles away. I decided to check for myself if they were still there. When I got to the top of Seminary Ridge I noticed the Confederate campfires in the distance had tripled in size. At this point, I decided to walk back to my room at once and pack. Many of our men were singing and many were writing, most likely home to a loved one before going into what could be their last battle. As I turned and walked toward the Eagle Hotel, I observed a circle of men engaged in prayer, asking the Father in Heaven for protection and care if they should see battle tomorrow. I silently asked the Good Lord the same thing as I walked back and retired for the evening.

Jennie (Ginnie) Wade
Courtesy of the Gettysburg Museum of History

July 1, 1863 – 1st day of battle

Morning arrived, but I must admit I really did not sleep a wink with the Confederate Army in such close proximity. Outside my window, I heard on the street below men and horses passing by in a rush most of the night. They seemed to be heading west up the Chambersburg Street toward the Seminary and south down Washington Street. The commotion really made a racket. I decided to pack my bags, thinking this confusion might offer me a chance to return home. After thinking some more on the subject, I realized that was a foolish idea. Here was the story of a lifetime and it was unfolding right in front of me. It would be foolish to walk away from this opportunity. I flashbacked in my mind to the aggressive reporter that I always had been – fearless and unafraid to be in harm's way in the face of danger for the chance to get a story. This was my job, my livelihood, what I was being paid to do!

I walked down to the lobby; there were soldiers all over the place. As I walked along Chambersburg Street, I began to worry about Chester. I couldn't let any harm come to my horse; besides me, my wife would be heartbroken if we were to lose him. I stopped by my friend Charles Tyson's Photography Studio; it was packed with soldiers wanting to get their photo taken. I asked Charles if he knew of a safe place I could keep Chester. "I'm really busy right now," he said, "but this farmer is in town and is taking what is left of his livestock after the Rebs confiscated most of it on the 26th up into the hills. He might be able to help you." I bid Charles a good day; he was so busy I don't think he even knew I left. I found the farmer and he wanted thirty dollars to take care of Chester adding that I would have to pay him another twenty dollars upon Chester's safe return. I knew it was a very steep price, but my wife and I are really fond of Chester. The farmer then said he would not guarantee his safe return.

On hearing that, I told him I would make other arrangements. I didn't trust this fellow with my horse anyway; he seemed like someone who would take advantage of a stranger. I told him to forget it because of the way he looked at Chester; I knew he was not to be trusted with my horse.

I heard shots in the distance, so the battle must have begun. What should I do or go if the Confederate artillery shells the town! I rode back to Charles' studio although he had a crowd there earlier and I knew he was busy. "Charles, Charles," I called as I entered the studio. He appeared nervous as he came out from the darkroom. "Where did all those soldiers go?" he asked. "The place is empty; you'd better come with me," he continued, "and bring Chester! Hurry!" I ran and grabbed Chester and followed him down the road to his house. I helped Charles load up a wagon and then helped Maria into it; Maria then looked at me and screamed. "The trunk, we need to get the trunk!" Charles and Maria had stored a trunk with their neighbor Mr. Boyer, he was dragging it out as we spoke, pulling it towards the wagon with an elderly woman behind him, not sure if it was Mister Boyer's mother. Charles and I hoisted the trunk up among the other trunks on Mr. Boyer's wagon; I thought the wagon belonged to Charles originally. " I asked Maria, "What do you have in there?" Maria said, "My wedding gown, no Rebel is going to steal it from me." For a second, all three of us looked at one another and not a word was uttered but I think Maria knew what we were thinking. Charles finally said, "Tie Chester to the wagon. Don't worry, I'll look after him for you." I thanked and hugged them both for taking Chester and for being such dear friends. They begged me to go with them but I decided it was my duty to stay in town and write down all I witnessed. I started back toward the sound of the fighting. Maria yelled, "Be careful and God bless" as they rode out of sight!

I can hear more gunshots in the distance. They seem to have increased and are moving closer to town. Like most people, I suspect the Rebels are coming from the direction of Cashtown; however, another pedestrian speculated that most of General Lee's army is still at Chambersburg. I noticed many in town were closing up their shops. People were running to their homes. That's when it happened - a large boom...then another and another. I soon lost count. This was it—the battle for Gettysburg had begun. As I ran up Chambersburg Street, I noticed a Union soldier being dragged on the ground past me by his horse with his one foot caught in the stirrup. Mister Burns grabbed the bridle of the horse, bringing it to a stop. Looking down, Mr. Burns cut the soldier loose from the horse with a knife. Mr. Burns looked up at me with the angriest look a man of sixty-nine could give and yelled, "That cuts it, by God, that's the last straw!" He went into his house and minutes later came out with an old flintlock musket and dressed in a coat from another decade. I didn't know what to say as he walked right past me like I wasn't there. Then he yelled to Joe Broadhead, "Ya coming Joe?" Mr. Broadhead stepped out his door and said nothing. Mr. Burns then waved his hand in disgust and exclaimed, "Cowards, a town of cowards!" and proceeded to walk toward the Seminary. Mrs. Burns stuck her head out the window and yelled, "John, you get back here!" But the old man just kept walking and grumbling under his breath.

I ran up Chambersburg Street after Mister Burns but stopped at the Seminary out of fear. As he continued to walk toward the smoke and gunshots out of sight, I could see the battle unfolding before my eyes. There was smoke everywhere. I was excited and terrified at the same moment and quickly started to scribble down notes as fast as I could. A voice called out, "Hey mister, you had better leave here, it's not safe!" "And you are?" I asked. "I am Emmanuel Ziegler and am the steward of the Seminary." Just then a group of men on horseback rode by. "It looks like one of them is a general," Mr. Ziegler said. "Yes, yes I know who he is," I said. "He is General John Reynolds with his staff, he is the Union Infantry Commander of the 1st Corps!" Mr. Ziegler and I returned smiles at one another because we knew General Reynolds was one of the best generals in the Union Army. I told him I appreciated his concern for me and that I would be leaving shortly. I also told him that I was a reporter and wanted to make a few more observations in my notes. "Okay then," he said, "just make sure they aren't the last notes you ever write!" I thanked him and walked closer to the action. I could see men with axes knocking down fences right behind me looking back toward the town, they were soldiers of the 1st Corps approaching the fighting, I believe led by General Wadsworth from photographs I have seen. They reinforced our cavalry, which had been fighting so very hard for hours.

Soldiers with tall black hats moved right into the woods in front of us. They were part of the famed Iron Brigade of the 1st Corps and they were known as hard fighters. The firing had intensified now that our infantry had joined the cavalry. They will show those Rebs a thing or two, I vowed. It looked like General Buford and his staff were in the cupola of the Seminary yelling down to General Reynolds and his staff, who now moved with the 1st Brigade forward. I looked in amazement at the Colonel of the Iron Brigade who was also wearing the tall black hat, he seemed to be the tallest man I had ever seen. They called to him; I think I heard them say Colonel Meredith, but am unsure.

The fighting was escalating. I was warned by many an officer to "Get out of here" and now maybe I will heed that advice. I decided to take one more look. Oh my, is that Mister Burns? He is fighting right alongside some of the soldiers. He has to be one of the bravest sixty-nine year old men in the world! I started to run down Chambersburg Street back into town; it seemed like people were all on the rooftops watching what was taking place. Cannonballs were heard whizzing overhead. What are these people thinking? What does it take to go to your cellars and get out of harm's way? What am I saying, I'll bet they are saying the same thing about me! I then heard from a distance someone yell, "Women and children to your cellars, they are going to shell the town!"

I looked back toward the Seminary when I saw the wounded starting to stagger into town; I think I heard some of them say that General Reynolds had been killed, I pray that is not true and hope they are wrong, for he is one of our finest generals. I came to Washington Street and new infantry was approaching. It appeared to be the Union 11th Corps. When I tried to cross the street through the infantry line many of the soldiers pushed me back and yelled, "Get out of der vay!" I believe they were German but I didn't stick around to find out. I couldn't cross the street back to my hotel and I can clearly see it across the street? I will have to find another way through this confusion to get back to the Eagle Hotel to retrieve my belongings. I noticed a woman come out her front door to see what was going on when an artillery shell crashed into her rear balcony. She looked at me and ran back into the house. What a look she had, almost as if she had seen a ghost…she was terrified. I passed more and more wounded soldiers on my way through town until they were too numerous to count. I wandered around observing a mass of soldiers, bloodied and beaten, heading back from the Seminary. I saw a soldier limping alone toward the center of town falling twice. I then ran up to him and said, "Let me help you." As he raised his head, I saw that he could not have been a day over eighteen years old. He had been shot in the thigh and hand covered in blood with a gunpowder blackened face. I could see his eyes full of tears and I will remember that boy's eyes for the rest of my life. I quickly helped him up and across the street into the church that Mr. Burns had referred to as the "College Church." A woman rushed over and helped me. Later; I found out that her name was Mary McAllister. We laid that young soldier down on a pew. We told the surgeon this soldier needed help but he snapped back, "Hey mister, I have a hundred men that need me. See what you can do until I get to him." I found a long ribbon and we told him we were going to tie it around his leg to stop the bleeding. I just kept hoping that I was doing the right thing since I had never before helped a wounded person and had no medical knowledge. I also wrapped my handkerchief around his hand to stop the bleeding. The soldier thanked me and told me he was with the 147th New York Infantry and that he was hit as soon as the fighting started. "It seemed that we were out in the open when we were attacked," he said. "I don't think General Wadsworth wanted us to be in the open like that," he continued. "We were dropping like flies and that's when I was hit. Colonel Miller ordered me and about six others to get into town and find the surgeon. It was so loud and confusing. Mister, I am in so much pain, am I going to die?" he asked. For a moment I was speechless, not knowing what to say. I finally answered, "No of course not, you will be allright" and added that he should rest as the surgeon will soon get to him and properly dress his wounds. I told him I must leave but I would return to see him. Miss McAllister said she would stay as she only lives across the street. I wished him well and started to the door.

A man to my left had one of his legs torn off at the knee, a ghastly wound. He appeared to be in shock. As I prepared to leave the church, I heard him ask for water. I could not leave this helpless man, so I gave him some water from a discarded canteen I found on the pew next to him. He drank what little water was inside; smiled slightly and then he passed out as they bandaged his wound. I asked the orderly who appeared to be part of the Iron Brigade what happened to him. He shook his head and said, "Those soldiers say that fella there thought he was smart, trying to stop a rolling cannonball with his foot; I bet he never does that again"…I tried to envision the incident but could not help feeling pity for the man.

I left the church. It was then I noticed the streets were now absent of most civilians. Soldiers in blue, wagons and horses were hurriedly coming through town from all directions; it was total confusion. I could see people looking out their windows, a few civilians passing out water with buckets and dippers, but many I assumed, went to their cellar for protection. I could hear the sound of cannon shells passing overhead. Men shouted, " Head for the cemetery on the hill." I don't know how anyone will reach it with all this confusion in town; the firing was getting heavy again. So many wounded were coming into town and I asked myself, "Where will they go?" The wave of blue moved down the streets, many would enter or be carried into homes, businesses, even placed under the shade of trees. The cries and moans were heart wrenching. Just then a shell hit the Christ Lutheran Church, which I had just left. Now I was worried and I am not afraid to say, downright scared! I pray Miss McAllister and that young soldier were not harmed.

I tried to make my way across the street to my hotel and I was caught up in the mass of blue running through the town with cannon shells bursting all around. As we ran through the diamond of town and turning right down Baltimore Street, I had no choice but to go with the flow of men. I tripped over discarded army packs and muskets and was almost trampled to death like a herd of cattle running through town. I crawled toward the side of the road lucky to still be alive. Just then I heard a boy call out, "Hey mister, hey mister reporter, OVER HERE!" I crawled toward the voice while being stepped on and kicked. I looked up; it was my young friend Albertus McCreary, standing at the side of the road with others holding a bucket of water and dipper passing out water. "Albertus, get inside the house NOW!" A man I believed to be his father yelled. "C'mon mister," Albertus said. "You're better off inside as well." His father waved us in and slammed the door shut. "Everyone in the cellar," said the man who I later found out was Albertus' father, David McCreary. I tried to introduce myself but Mr. McCreary said, "My boy told me all about you at Winter's Candy Store, but now is not the time to talk." We went to the cellar and it was full of terrified people; luckily it was large enough to accommodate everyone. Albertus was holding a large drum. I looked at him puzzled and asked, "What do you have there?" He answered, "A drum." He then added that a Union drummer boy handed him his drum and told Albertus to hide it and that he will come back for it.

Those were the last words spoken in that cellar for a while as we all stared at a small window. We saw hundreds of men in blue run by. Then, for a few minutes, the streets seemed empty. Suddenly, a large boom was heard. A cannon had been fired right in the middle of the street. The house shook and we heard dishes falling off the shelves upstairs. Then as we watched that window and saw hundreds of men running by, but they were wearing GREY! The enemy had taken the town! They ran after our boys in blue. The Rebels were hollering and yelling; it was terrifying as they passed by the window. We heard a Rebel scream, "Shoot 'em! Shoot 'em! Shoot that Yankee!" A shot was heard. I felt sympathy for the poor soldier who was the intended target, for I fear he was killed running for safety.

Then, the sound of musket fire seemed to be coming from the cemetery area. We all sat there quietly for a while and then suddenly the cellar doors were pulled open. Albertus jumped up and some of the women screamed and cried. "Any Yanks down here?" a red haired Reb with a big bushy beard shouted." He was with about four or five others, all dirty and dust covered and sweaty. Nobody said a word and the soldiers just stood there. I don't believe they knew what to do, but I was never so close to an actual Confederate soldier not to mention one pointing a gun at me. At that point Mr. McCreary stepped forward and said, "Gentlemen, this is my house and we are all citizens of this town (bless his heart, I thought, for I was simply a guest in town) and we are unarmed." "Well mister, we are looking for Union soldiers, any down here?" he asked. "No," Mr. McCreary replied. "There are no soldiers in this house." "Well, we have to look anyways, get them upstairs," the soldier motioned to the other soldiers with him. When we got upstairs, those Confederate soldiers rounded up about twelve or thirteen Union soldiers, we didn't hear those Union soldiers enter and go up to the second floor. Everyone was taken to the dining room. Then something happened that, if I did not write it down, I wouldn't have believed it myself. Only in war could such a strange incident happen. Mr. McCreary looked at all the soldiers in the room, Union and Confederate and asked, "Gentlemen, would you care for something to eat?" I wondered if he was doing this out of the kindness of his heart or because he had just told them there were no soldiers in the house and they found those Union soldiers hiding

For whatever reason, it was a brilliant move. The food was already on the table before the Confederate Army took over the town and Mrs. McCreary brought out some more. And to my amazement, everyone sat down together and was eating like Sunday dinner back home. Albertus asked me for a piece of paper to write down all the Union soldiers names. The red-haired Rebel made a joke and everyone in the room laughed. How strange is war. An hour before, these two groups of men were shooting and killing one another and now are eating and laughing together as if they were at one big family get-together. Then the Confederates left escorting their Union prisoners to the rear. Everyone remaining in the house lay where they were and slept out of pure exhaustion, for it was dark and very humid outside due to all the smoke in the air. I rested my head on my ledger and went to sleep, grateful for making it safely through the day.

July 2, 1863 – 2nd Day of Battle

I woke up and it was dawn. I was a little embarrassed because I saw that I was the last person to awaken from the previous day at the McCreary home. These folks must wonder what kind of reporter I am if I sleep with so much going on outside. I looked around and not surprisingly my little friend Albertus was gone. I doubt the Rebels would do any harm to him, being only a fifteen-year-old civilian boy. I could hear intermittent gunshots, probably from sharpshooters in the upstairs rooms of surrounding houses. Mrs. McCreary gave me a piece of warm bread with preserves. I am not exaggerating when I say it was the most delicious piece of bread I had ever eaten, so I was sure to thank Mrs. McCreary for her kindness.

Just then we heard a large commotion at the front of the house. Everyone ran to the front and saw two Confederates take Albertus by the arms. "Wait," Mr. McCreary said. "What are you doing?" The officer shouted out, "He is in the Union Army and he is coming with us." Mr. McCreary laughed, "He is only a school boy." It was amazing how calm and composed Mr. McCreary was in the face of danger. I really admired him for that as well as keeping everyone in his house safe. The officer still insisted Albertus was with the Union Army and then everyone in the house and the neighbors came running over and insisted he was a civilian. I think since all these people were insisting, the officer was persuaded to let him go. It appeared Albertus would have far greater problems when his father gets him inside after that incident. I saw Mr. McCreary grow perturbed with what had just unfolded before him and poor Albertus ran upstairs as fast as he could. Trouble just seems to follow that young man.

I thanked Mister McCreary for his hospitality, shook his hand and took my leave. I wanted to try to make my way back to the Eagle Hotel to see if any of my clothes and supplies were still there. Being a guest in this town, I had no responsibility for a home, family or business that might be burglarized or ransacked by the Confederate Army, I am going to see if I could be of some help to the wounded for I know many are suffering.

I started up Baltimore Street staring at all the dead soldiers and horses lying in the streets when I was stopped by two ragged looking Rebs at the point of a musket. "Where ya going mister?" they asked. "I am headed to the Eagle Hotel," I responded in a soft voice, continuing, "I was traveling through Pennsylvania when I was caught up in this battle." The two men paused and looked at each other. "Traveler, huh? You just stand there," he said while the other man brought over a soldier who appeared to be a captain. "Who are you mister, ya live on this here street and where are you off to?" he asked. I told him I was a reporter and at that point he stopped me mid-sentence asking, "You aren't with that New York paper, are you? They wrote that our General Early burned down that town we were in and that was the furthest thing from the truth. We helped put that fire out and that was the thanks we got from some two-bit Yankee newspaper!" I told him I was from Pennsylvania and in town to visit a friend. He told me that General Lee is marching to Washington and I could report that to all the Yankee newspapers up north. He told me I couldn't go to the hotel because of the fighting that happened around it yesterday. "Those Yankees were holed up in the houses around the hotel as well as shooting out of the hotel windows." He continued, "We surrounded the block until one of the officers from a New York regiment came out under parley and saw the situation was hopeless and surrendered. We were going to parole that fellow, a German fellow and could you believe, I could barely understand a damn word he said, what I could make out was he wouldn't accept parole and he would make it difficult for us and impede our progress. I know the major over there and he was going to run him through with a bayonet. I have to admit it took gumption for that German fellow to say what he said in the face of death". I was later told this German officer was Captain Francis Irsch of the 45th New York Infantry.

After telling him I was a newspaper reporter, this officer from Georgia told me to tie a white cloth around my arm if I was going to walk around town but told me it would be better to stay inside for my own safety as there are sharpshooters all over town and it would not be wise to be in the line of fire. I could hear bullets whizzing overhead and an occasional shell explode. He also told me he is involved with a small newspaper back home and would most likely be doing the same thing I was in looking for a story. He told me he had to go but added not to wander around. "Some of these fellows might not take too kindly to you, especially those fellows from Louisiana." I thanked him and went on my way. I wish I knew what he meant about those soldiers from Louisiana? But I sure hope I never cross paths with them.

But where was I going, as I kept walking up the street? This was a very dangerous affair, I thought. And I am not that familiar with the town and now the Confederates occupy it. With Union bullets occasionally whizzing around town, I walked back toward the Eagle Hotel by way of Middle Street. I feared that all my supplies had been stolen from my room but maybe with some luck I might retrieve something of mine that might not have been taken. As I walked up High Street and came to St. Francis Xavier Church, I noticed a young lady crying on the steps of the church. "Are you all right Miss?" I asked. She wiped the tears from her eyes, shook her head yes and went into the church wiping her eyes. I decided to follow her since I was interested in seeing what she was so upset about. I had recognized her from a few days ago handing out bread when our cavalry rode through town. I believe she told me her name was Miss Sallie Myers. With all the projectiles whizzing around town, I thought it couldn't hurt to be inside for I was not anxious to become a target.

Salome "Sallie" Myers
Picture courtesy of the Adams County Historical Society

As I entered the church, I saw Miss Myers kneeling down next to a wounded sergeant, wiping the sweat from his brow. I noticed wince of pain in his face and his eyes welled up with tears. I must admit that my eyes were not short of tears as well due to the moans and cries of the wounded soldiers, but I had a job to do and started to write what I saw. Then I saw something so beautiful and innocent. It was very moving and I struggled to keep my composure. Miss Myers was reading from a Bible to the wounded sergeant, "Let not your heart be troubled, ye believe in God. In my Father's house are many mansions, if it were not so, I would have told you. I go to prepare a place for you." As she continued to read, the sergeant stared at the ceiling smiling, as if to visualize what Sallie had just read to him, it comforted him in some way. That sight I will never forget. For through all this killing and cruel butchery and death all around, this small gesture from this dear young lady must have made this poor soldier realize maybe this war was something that was worth possibly giving his life for and most likely the lives of his men.

"Hey mister," yelled a doctor, tapping me on my shoulder, "if you're not helping, get out of the way!" I hesitated, then asked, "What can I do, doctor?" "Go over there with this bucket of water and give 'em a drink; a lot of them are crying for water," he said. Grabbing the bucket from the doctor, I moved toward the front of the church. I was told the doctor's name was Dr. Fulton. As I drew closer to the wounded, I knew I was going to see some horrible sights. I thought to myself that I had never been around a dead or dying man, how would I react? When I saw these poor wounded men lying across the pews, under the pews and sitting up along the walls, begging me for water, my fear left my body. I started to give them water when I saw Union and Confederate soldiers mixed together! How is it that these men were just killing one another and now lying side by side? It reminded me of the incident at the McCreary house yesterday when Union and Confederates were eating and laughing at the same table. How strange is war, I thought.

I discovered some of the men were from New York, Pennsylvania and Wisconsin - the regiments I don't remember. Some of the Confederates were from Tennessee and North Carolina. I am sure there were men from other states as well. Another sight I would remember was when I handed the ladle of water to a big, thirsty captain from New York with a wound to his leg. He then handed it to a young wounded Confederate who was about fourteen years old. This boy was weeping and saying, "I want to go home." "There, there," the Union captain said. "Drink up!" He handed the ladle to the boy and told him, "It will be all right son, don't cry." After the wounded boy drank, the thirsty captain took the ladle and had his drink. Could this Union soldier have a son the same age? Or was it the mere act of kindness showing the enemy mercy in this House of God? Whatever the case, our country could learn so much from this simple act of kindness.

I continued giving the wounded men water. My bucket was soon completely dry, so I went to find another bucket of water or refill this one. It was then that I saw a very disturbing sight, a pile of arms and legs about three feet high next to where the surgeons were working on the wounded and there was blood everywhere! I froze where I stood. "My God," I said aloud, staring at the pile. "Move it, move it mister! I have wounded to attend," said the surgeon as he pushed me aside. As I started to walk past this ghastly sight, I saw a Union soldier on the table the surgeons were working on. He looked as if he had been shot through the knee. I could see three men holding him down while the surgeon took hold of his leg. I knew as well as this young soldier, who looked no older than twenty years old, what was to come next. As I walked by, the young soldier turned his head while lying on that table, his eyes meeting mine. We both stared at each other for what seemed like an eternity. His eyes welled up with tears as he tensed his body. I could see his lips quivering with fear with anticipation of the next act, which was about to happen. I will never forget the look of terror on that poor young soldier's face. I walked away in shame for not staying with this helpless soul and trying to comfort him. I could hear his screams in the background. I could hear him begging them to stop. I said aloud, "My God, my God, please help this poor young man in his suffering. Oh, please Lord, help him." At that moment his screams stopped, for the act of removing his leg had ended. I could hear him moaning in pain and at that moment I began to cry like I never have before. I have never been in such a horrific place like this in my life. Flies, dirt and blood were everywhere, even on my hands and trousers and the cry of the surgeons, "NEXT, NEXT, NEXT!" was constant and something that will forever haunt me. That was all I could endure; I had to get out of there before I lost all my sanity.

St. Francis Xavier Catholic Church
Courtesy of the Adams County Historical Society

I left the church and headed back toward Baltimore Street paying no attention to my surroundings and forgetting that the town was occupied and that there was a war going on outside the church. I was just a few feet away from Baltimore Street, when all of a sudden I heard, "Halt or I'll shoot!" I slowly turned to see two Confederates aiming at my head. "Who are ya mister?" asked the young Confederate. "I am just returning from the church, where I was helping with the wounded," I said. "Aw, he's all right, Jim," said the other soldier. Still pointing his gun, the first soldier asked, "Where do you live mister and how do we know you're not a bushwhacker?" "A bushwhacker, what's a bushwhacker?" I asked. "Don't get smart with me mister. You know it's someone that's a fightin' and dressed like a civilian!" he cried. I assured the soldiers, "I am no bushwhacker and I doubt there are any in this town." He put the muzzle of the gun closer to my head and said, "Callin' me a liar, mister? I don't take lip from no Yankee lover!" Then an officer approached and said, "What goes here, Private?" "Sir," he answered, "this here Yankee says there ain't no bush- whackers around these parts but them boys from North Carolina said they found that old man fighting with the Yankees up there on the hill." "That's right," said the officer, "that old fool told our captain he was getting some girl to help with his sick wife, but told me ten minutes later he was looking for his cow! Dang fool was hit three times, so he can rot for all I care" I apolo- gized for my mistake about the bushwhacker and told them I was a reporter for a newspaper up north and wanted to report on the battle. "A newspaper reporter?" the officer laughed, "Ha ha, get a load of this, if that don't beat all!" The original angry soldier said, "I got a story for ya - ask your readers if they like the way General Lee and the Army of Northern Virginia came back into the Union." A loud roar of laughter went up from the group. I must admit I was scared, but what they said next scared the daylights out of me. "We here are Louisiana Tigers, so write that down mister." I remembered what that soldier from Georgia had said earlier about those boys from Louisiana. "A newspaperman?" said one of the other soldiers. "You ain't from that newspaper up north that's always tellin' lies about us, are ya? I might have to put one right between your eyes, Mister Newspaper Man!" "No sir, I report it fair," I continued. "I am for the Union I admit, but I have relatives in the South, so I would like to hear from you boys as well." "I don't know if we believe ya mister. You could be making that up to save your hide; tell us a little more about the south," he taunted. After about an hour of blurting out everything I knew about the south, they began to believe me. "Hey Private," said a sergeant in the group, "go take this reporter fella back to see those fellas in General Rodes' division. We gotta move, General Early gave orders to move toward that hill up yonder." I thought to myself, if I ever make it out of here I would never take a job with that New York Newspaper after all the trouble it caused me.

I was escorted back up High Street. Bullets were whizzing overhead. We passed the Catholic Church and out in front was a group of orderlies carrying a stretcher with what looked to be a soldier with the rank of sergeant, it was that same fellow I saw earlier in the church and along side holding his hand was Miss Myers, the same young lady who earlier was crying on the steps of the church. She looked up and smiled. The soldier was in excruciating pain but continued to look at Miss Myers as if she were an angel of the Lord sent to comfort him. They entered a house nearby, maybe it was the Myers home, but I could not be sure, I was escorted closer to Washington Street through more yards to avoid any errant bullets meant for a Confederate sharpshooter. We ended up back on Chambersburg Street. I was told to sit down and don't move while this private told about thirty Confederate soldiers sitting in a group about capturing me when all of a sudden they all turned around and gave me the same stare. I asked what was going to happen to me and received the retort, "Hush up, we will be asking the questions here not you!"

Looking around I was shocked at all the carnage on the street. Union knapsacks and haversacks no doubt thrown away by soldiers during the retreat through town yesterday lay everywhere. I saw some Confederates looking through them and laughing at some of the contents. One pulled out a picture and was showing it to the group when an officer admonished him and told him to place all of the items in a pile. I could see dead soldiers and bloated dead horses on the sides of the street. It was a sight and smell I will never forget. The officer told me to get up. "What are you doing roaming around town, son?" he asked. I explained I was a visitor to town and had been helping the wounded at the Catholic Church. "Well, that's good mister," he answered, "Now get in that church over there and help out; it isn't safe to be out in the open." I moved slowly until another Reb said, "Now get!" as he shoved me in the back.

Once again I was in church, this time it was the church the locals call the College Church - Christ Lutheran to be exact. I ran across a captain who laid motionless, blood all over his long white gloves. I went up to him and prodded him. To my regret, he must have already died. An orderly came over and said, "Grab his legs, mister and let's move him to the back of the church." As I carried this man, I imagined this soldier ripe with pride joining the army to fight for a cause he had so strongly believed in and now he is dead and being placed with so many other young heroes side by side. I thought to myself, what a tremendous waste of life. These men could have been poets or doctors or inventors who could have changed all of our lives, but now they are dead with nothing more to give mankind. I think of how many mothers and wives sit in silent prayer asking God to bring their loved ones home safely, not knowing their loved ones have met their end in a small town in Pennsylvania. So sad, so very sad, I thought to myself.

I had just finished that thought when all kinds of artillery opened up. Musketry fire was heard in the distance. This continued for hours. I decided I was safe right here and the wounded seemed to keep trickling in. It was getting late. I continued to give the wounded men water (I was becoming good at this). Outside, you could still hear shooting but it was coming from Cemetery Hill and not from the south where I believe Reverend Sherfy said he lived. I needed to write all this down and get some sleep; I was totally exhausted. I sat down in the corner of the church and fell asleep among all those wounded men, still holding my pad and pencil in my hands.

July 3, 1863 – 3ʳᵈ day of battle

I awoke to gunfire in the distance, then a loud voice shaking me demanding, "Get up, get up, we need this spot!" I picked myself up and went to the steps of the church; my neck as stiff as a board from the position I had slept in and it seemed to be the start of a very hot and humid day. I had awakened hoping that the Rebs would have left town, but to my disappointment they had not. A small group of Confederates were standing and talking in front of the church. I remembered to wear my white armband in plain view. I walked up to them and they all looked at me. One of the men asked, "What is your business here, Yank? Get moving or my boot will find your backside!" An officer in their group told the arrogant soldier to "Shut it." He then told them all, "This is still their town."

I asked, "Where was the fighting taking place?" Another soldier asked, "What's it to you? Are you some sort of spy?" Now, I don't know if it was because I was tired or just hungry but all I wanted to do is make conversation so I said, "A spy? Are you joking? I am a reporter and I just asked a simple question and could do without all the insults you men may have. You come into this town, steal, pay with your worthless money and insult us. I have family in the South and they are polite and friendly, not rude like some of the Confederate soldiers I have encountered." I appeared steamed on the outside but I was terrified on the inside. I thought to myself "I'm as good as dead." They stood there with an angry look and then moved toward me. Then that same officer told me, " Look here Mr. Reporter, let me tell you about how the Yankees came into Fredericksburg and stole everything some folks owned and then destroyed what was left. It was them that started the stealing and looting. Write that down and let the people now the truth! We Confederates could have burned this town to the ground and taken everything. All you people

owe General Lee a might big 'thank you' for his orders."
He then added, "The Yankees wish they had an officer as
smart and caring as our great General Lee." Another soldier added, "No Yankee general could hold General Lee's
hat and that also includes your Uncle Abe!" I didn't know
what to say. I asked, "Are you sure Union soldiers did that in
Fredericksburg?" "Are you kidding me, mister?" came the
response. "You think they are all angels. Well, they ain't.
Go talk to some of the boys from Virginia; they'll tell ya so!
Some lost everything they had as well as some kin!"

The officer spoke up again and asked, "So where are ya
going anyways, Mr. Reporter, ya going to see who else's skin
ya can get under? Go see those Louisiana boys; they'll eat ya
up for lunch." I looked around and spotted Miss McAllister
talking to two Confederates in the front of her house. I told
the officer that I was going over to her residence to see if
I could be of any assistance with the wounded. I also told
them I did not know about the events in Fredericksburg, but
I would remember what they told me. As I walked across
the street, I could not believe I had left that group alive but
I had and was grateful I did without a bruise. I walked to
Miss McAllister's home and my nose caught the aroma of
something wonderful. It was the scent of a pie coming off
of the windowsill and I was drawn to it like a fly to a sugar
cake. The two soldiers refused Miss McAllister's offer of
a piece of pie. "What?" I thought to myself, "I would give
a weeks pay for a piece of that pie. Why would they refuse
it?" I heard one of them say, "I ain't going to die over a piece
of pie." "We don't poison people here in Gettysburg," Miss
McAllister snapped back. " I cannot believe you think I poisoned it; shame on you!" she exclaimed. "Let's go. I don't
trust her," the other soldier said. Miss McAllister with her
hands on her hips, looked at me and asked, "Would you like
a poisoned piece of pie?" She smiled as she bit into a piece. I
answered, "There is nothing in the world I would like more,

ma'am." I thought to myself that if those two soldiers only knew what they were missing as I finished the delectable slice of pie. Mary McAllister, finishing her slice, grinned at me saying, "Martha makes the best pie in Adams County, maybe in the entire Union." After all I had been through and the rumble in my stomach, I just shook my head and said, "I totally agree. That was delicious!"

I started walking back towards the Eagle Hotel to make another attempt at retrieving my belongings, since it was only a few doors down, I was thinking to myself that I was pushing the odds against my survival, for the streets were void of civilians but full of Confederate soldiers moving up and down Chambersburg Street. I wondered what had become of Mr. Burns; did he survive and if so, was he badly wounded? Are Charles and Maria safe and what of my horse Chester? At this point I realized that although I was scared, I now had an obligation to survive this and tell the story of all that the town of Gettysburg as well as what I had endured. I surely hope I will be around to write the ending....

It was close to noon and again I was denied entry into the Eagle Hotel. In a rather rude way, the Rebel guard told me to "Git!" adding that he has orders to let no one in. It was being used as a hospital and it was not the welcoming hotel I knew when I first checked in. The stench of a dead horse in the street was beyond anything I could remember. I ran across the street to the church with my face buried in my handkerchief. Pausing, I looked down to see the face of a dead Union soldier. He looked no older than twenty years old. I froze as I realized he was on a pile of other dead soldiers stacked like cordwood and I could only imagine what these poor men faced in the final moments of their lives. It looked as if anyone entering this yard that was unable to scale the wall, had been shot and was placed in this pile of dead soldiers. All of a sudden I heard, "Hey you, get away from them dead Yankees unless you wanna join them!" As I turned around, I saw a young Confederate soldier with his rifle raised at my head. "What's your business here?" he asked. "I was just getting back to the Catholic Church to help with the wounded," I said. "Listen here," the cocky Rebel snapped, "I ain't pleased with you lookin at those dead Yankees; might think you want to rob 'em or somethin'!" Another soldier said, "What ya got in that bag mister? Hand it over." I realized I had no choice but told them I was a visitor in town and it was all I had so could I please keep my possessions so I might survive until I went home. The cocky Rebel snapped back, "Well mister, we are all visitors to this here town and this gun I am pointing at ya is all I have!" to the laughter of the few soldiers with him, "SO GIVE ME THE DAMN BAG!" As I started to remove the bag from around my shoulder I realized everything I had written was in this bag. What could I possibly say to keep my cherished items? Once again, as if my guardian angel was at my side looking over my every move, a Rebel on horseback came charging at the group holding me hostage yelling, "Get back here now!" The cocky Rebel yelled out, "It's that gal we stole molasses from, run, boys run!" As they ran an officer pursued them on horseback. I turned toward a few other Rebels that ran over and was shocked to see Miss McAllister was with them. "Don't worry ma'am, the captain will get them," a young soldier assured her and then walked back to stand guard at her house. I looked at Miss McAllister amazed and speechless. She turned to them and said, "Damn old bitch they called me, well I guess I showed them!" I thanked her for coming to my rescue and she said she complained about those misbehaving soldiers until their captain gave chase. She was carrying a pail and going to find some milk, but was not about to let that bunch off the hook for their rudeness. How happy I was for this brave woman to stand up for herself and with that gesture, also allowed me to keep my belongings. I thanked her again and as she walked away I noticed how she had clenched her fists in anger at the thought of how rude that young soldier had been. Boy, did they pick the wrong lady to mess with!

As I continued walking toward the Catholic Church, I heard a tapping from a window of a nearby house. It was Professor Jacobs. "Quick, come in, hurry," he called. I entered the living room of the house. Thanking him for letting me find refuge in his home, I asked if he knew what was happening, for at that moment the Confederates were hurrying up and down the streets as if a beehive had been kicked next to them. "I don't know," he said. "This is my son Henry and we have been watching the movement from the garret; but now, let us get to the cellar." "No father, I want to see this for myself," young Henry said. He looked to be about eighteen years old and I totally understood how he felt. You wait here mister," he said. "We will be right back." I remained in the cellar while they walked back up the stairs when all of a sudden it sounded like the heavens had opened up. I had never heard the amount of cannon fire nor do I think I ever will again, like I did on this day July 3rd 1863. I looked at my watch and it was one o'clock in the afternoon. The booming of the cannon went on for hours one after another, the ground never shook so hard. I thought to myself, how could anyone withstand that barrage of fire? Who was winning? Then the cannon fire slowed and now it was small arms fire. It was the most intense fighting of the three days. I could hear music in the background and wondered just what was going on? Here I am a reporter and I should be out there observing, but with all the dangerous situations and places I had been in these last few days, common sense prevailed and I stayed in that cellar.

I could hear footsteps; and hoped it was Professor Jacobs and Henry. The footsteps were getting closer and closer. The door opened....whew! It was the Professor and Henry. Professor Jacobs said it was something he would never forget, the cannons and the soldiers. Henry sat there and said nothing. He had witnessed something no other eighteen year old had witnessed and it must have troubled him from his reaction and silence. I asked what they saw. Professor Jacobs said, "The Confederates opened up with their artillery and the Union Army returned fire, it went on for two hours, then the Confederate Infantry started marching toward the Union line. It was real hard with all the smoke but we saw them march through open fields with their flags flying in a line toward Cemetery Hill. The Union artillery opened up holes in their ranks, but they kept coming. They reached and climbed the fence along the Emmitsburg Road and were dropping from the intense fire of the Union Army behind the wall on Cemetery Ridge. As the two armies merged into a hand-to-hand battle, many Confederate soldiers thought the better of it and ran back towards the woods from where they started. He said he could not imagine the amount of dead and dying lying on that field. The smoke had been so thick that it eventually obstructed their view and they could not see anything so they decided to return to the cellar. The Professor put his arm around Henry who appeared very upset and told him it would be all right.

Those poor souls, I thought to myself. Not three days ago they were in camp, writing loved ones, yearning to get home and continue the lives they had before this terrible war started and now they are laying wounded or dead in a field. How terrible is war and think of all those who perished today and all the possible contributions to mankind they will never make. From medicine to art to engineering, all those wasted lives now lie in a field never to be heard from again. We went upstairs and sat at Professor Jacobs' table talking about the day's events. By now, it was nighttime and the Confederates were moving up the street at a very quick pace. It seemed funny but they hardly made any noise doing so, almost as if they were leaving town and didn't want the Union Army to know. I knew the best place for me was right here on that floor where I was forever thankful for the kindness of Professor Jacobs. It didn't take long for me to fall into a sound sleep.

July 4, 1863

I awoke from that deep sleep to hear loud voices and wagons passing frantically in front of the house. It looked as if they were in a total state of confusion. It was raining and those wagons were racing towards the Seminary. I moved toward the window to see groups of Confederate soldiers running behind those wagons. They had been beaten yesterday, hurrah! I thought. It occurred to me the irony of the situation, for it was the 4th of July, Independence Day. I was writing with great excitement and not realizing I was standing in front of that window. It suddenly hit me that I could have been a sitting duck if, God forbid, a Rebel wanted to shoot one last Yankee before leaving town and I made the perfect target standing there. Once again, I thanked the Lord for giving me a wake up call to move away from that position.

I sat on the floor by the door reviewing my notes when someone tapped me on the shoulder. It startled me so much that I clean near hit the ceiling! I turned around to see Professor Jacobs standing there and snapped, "Please don't do that again Professor! I almost jumped out of my skin!" "Oh I am sorry, my good man," he replied, "but you appear to be a little too close to that door. It is not a safe place to compile your notes." I told him of my theory that the Rebels were possibly leaving town as I pointed to all the movement along Middle Street. My excitement was uncontrollable as more soldiers ran past the house, but Professor Jacobs remained silent. I asked him, "Professor, are you feeling all right? Why do you not share my excitement?" He looked at me with a smile and said, "My good fellow, the Confederate Army started to move out around 2 o'clock this morning. I have been watching the entire time. From my garret, I just saw the Union Army coming up Baltimore Street from the direction of the Wagon Hotel." I stood there with my mouth open and I said with a little anger in my voice, "Do you mean to tell me you have been watching this spectacle for hours and didn't wake me up?" "That's correct," he said, "you were sleeping so soundly I would tip toe past you so as not to wake you." I was at a loss for words. I was missing a reporter's dream of a story on one hand but on another the professor's fatherly instinct and kindness shown toward me was admirable; the fact that he did not want to wake me was touching. "I'm sorry, sir, for my tone of voice. Thank you," I said in a soft voice. As we both looked out the window, I added, "Now tell me EVERYTHING Professor!" with a smile. He looked back at me and chuckled and explained what he saw. Honestly, I think he was hoping I would ask him about all his diligent observations. As he was revealing his observations we saw a sight I will never forget; it was a group of Union soldiers coming up Middle Street. "Hurray!" we yelled, as a feeling of relief suddenly came over us. As the Union soldiers passed, I felt safe leaving the professor's house to explore this story that was unfolding before my eyes, I thanked the Professor for all the kindness he showed me and then I stepped out his front door when a shot hit right above my head. My goodness, I thought, on our first day of liberation, I was almost killed. The firing was picking up and the rain began to come down a bit harder; that smoky blue haze in the air seemed to dissipate with the falling rain.

Professor Michael Jacobs
Courtesy of the Adams County Historical Society

A young girl had wandered near the Professor's house curious of the situation when a bullet whizzed past her head. "Thank God she wasn't hit!" I thought. A man came running from one of the houses yelling "Mary!" Then he grabbed the child and ran into a yard belonging to a man that I later found out had the last name of Minnigh, as the Professor described it to me. He also said the girls name was Mary Warren and he felt relief upon seeing her not injured. Now unbeknownst to me, Henry Jacobs and his little sister also witnessed it and were horrified when a Union soldier was struck in the arm while on horseback crossing the very spot where Mary almost met her doom. A Confederate sharpshooter had his sights set on this location. Julia Jacobs began to yell to anyone approaching this spot, "Look out for the Rebel sharpshooters, for they will fire at you if they see you!" At that moment, several shots hit the door close to her, apparently trying to shut her up. The professor yelled, "Henry! Julia! Inside the house immediately!"

More Union soldiers moved around the house and returned fire. I believe the Rebels thought the better of it and moved closer to the Seminary area. The Union soldiers were setting up barricades all over and were here to stay, bless them. As I stood out in the rain evaluating my next move, I realized that those Rebel sharpshooters were out there and a bit trigger-happy, so I decided to stick to the cover of nearby homes. Our brave boys in blue were returning fire and gave me a great sense of security and confidence, so I moved from building to building and porch to porch. Because the completion of this story will be my big break in the newspaper field and I knew a few risks would be involved, but how many other reporters are in town doing what I'm doing? I just hope I don't do something stupid and get myself killed before I complete it.

As I looked back toward the cemetery, I could see lines of Confederate prisoners being led down the street; also, the shooting seemed to slow down, so maybe the battle was finally over. I decided to walk through some yards and realized I was close to John Burns' house. I wondered what happened to that old man, because if he survived, I wanted to be the first to interview him. I really hope he made it through the battle though, interview or not. Well, who am I kidding? I would love to conduct that interview more than anything in the world! I was more or less talking to myself and since I was daydreaming about that John Burns interview, I suddenly realized I was in a bad place, for I had wandered between the two battle lines of blue and gray. The quiet and calm was deafening. Just then I heard three shots whizzing by my head. THEY WERE SHOOTING AT ME! I dove behind a front porch and right into a puddle of water. I then crawled under the porch for safety. I can't believe it but I was almost killed and my nerves were getting the better of me. As I lay under a stranger's porch soaking wet and shaking, I looked to my right and noticed a small dog, which couldn't have been more than five or six months old staring back at me and was also shivering and soaking wet. I thought to myself that he must belong to the people living in this house. That pup was as terrified as I was.

In the front of the house I could hear the shots going back and forth and decided to wait it out right here, with the little dog I had just met. I was really hungry and I remembered I had some beef jerky in my coat pocket. Oh look who is moving closer to me, "C'mon boy, come here," I called. The little dog slowly moved toward me and took the jerky. "That's right, little fella, chew it good," I said. I decided to peek out from under the porch and could not see anything but could hear the occasional crack of gunfire and to make matters worse, the rain began to pour harder out of the sky. "Hey, save some for me!" I exclaimed when I realized the little dog had almost devoured all my jerky and I really needed some as well. For a moment, I stared at the dog and he stared back at me and I knew what was coming next…bark, bark, bark, his tail wagging. "Sssshhh," I whispered as I grabbed him and added, "Are you crazy, little dog? You are going to give our location away to the entire Confederate Army. Here, take the rest of it even if it is my last morsel of food." With the dog busy eating, I decided to make my move and run back into town as quickly as a reporter has ever run. I stood up and ran as fast as I ever have in my life and could see the Eagle Hotel ahead of me. The Confederate guns that had shot at me earlier now opened up on me again. I sought cover behind a tree just past the Eagle Hotel. Almost everyone else in town was inside, so where could I go? Just then, Miss McAllister stuck her head out her front door and called to me to come inside. Lucky for me I was close to her house. She must have seen my predicament and was offering me safety in her home, bless her soul. "Hurry, hurry," she said as I raced into her home through the door. I saw wounded soldiers laying on the floor, so I was careful not to step on them; some were very bad off with serious wounds. Miss McAllister asked if I could assist her with a young man who had been wounded at Mrs. Weikert's house and I said, "yes of course I will." Miss Mary still stood in the doorway with the door wide open. "What's wrong?" I asked. "Why are you standing in the doorway with the door wide open? Please Miss McAllister, close it, I would hate for you to be a target." She turned towards me and said, "I'm waiting for your little dog." I said, "I don't have a dog?" And in that moment who do you think came running through the door but the little pup that ate all my jerky. I asked Miss McAllister if she knew who he belonged to. "I have never seen him before," she said. "It looks like he has adopted you." I have to admit he was a cute little thing and lucky not to have been a target in his short journey to Miss McAllister's house. I had enough trouble keeping myself alive without watching out for a little pup, but what the heck, I knelt down and patted him on the head and he licked my face, while wagging his tail. I decided it was all right and told him to stay in the house while I helped Miss McAllister. I knew full well he had no clue what I was saying when a young wounded soldier said, "I'll watch him for you mister." You know, it did my heart good to see that poor wounded soldier laying there with wounds in both legs, holding the little pup and smiling as the pup licked his face. I think the pup loved the attention as well.

"We have to go right now," said Miss McAllister. We quickly ran to Mrs. Weikert's house a few doors away and found the young man lying by the door. Miss Mary and I lifted him up and got him inside. I believe he said his name was Amos and that he was a student at the Seminary. Once inside Mrs. Weikert and a very pretty young woman named Amanda started to tend his wound, he had been shot in the leg and with him safely inside I asked Miss Mary what we should do next? Mary said she should get back to her sister who is tending the wounded in their house all alone; and that the sight of blood would likely make her brother–in- law faint a second time. Mary lived with her sister and brother-in-law Martha and John Scott. She said that they had two Union officers upstairs in her house that should get to the hospital at Christ Lutheran Church. I offered my assistance and was wondering what had happened to all the men who had been there earlier in the battle. Mary with a sad look said, "Most of them were taken prisoner when the Confederates left the town. She also said she was not happy with the five Confederate surgeons who had set up quarters in her home. They demanded that Mary and her sister cook for them even though she would have rather aided the wounded. With the rain still coming down we made a dash back toward her house when suddenly a shot hit the building just over our heads. "The nerve of them!" Mary yelled out. "Come quick Miss McAllister," I said, "or I fear the next shot will hit its mark." We ran back into her house and were greeted at the door by that little pup, wagging his tail.

The wounded soldier who was watching him lifted his head slightly and asked, "What do you call him?" I was puzzled by the question and asked him what he meant. The wounded soldier asked, "What's the dog's name?" I smiled back at him and said that I had just found him no more than an hour ago, so I will have to think about it. At that moment, the little pup walked over to the soldier and lay down next to him. The soldier was so badly wounded from the loss of blood that he could barely lift his arm, but with great agony he put it around the pup and they both fell into a deep sleep.

Miss McAllister signaled me into the kitchen and told me she had to beg for that wounded soldier to remain in her home because of the severity of his wounds. She said she fears for him as he seems to be fading quickly and she fears he will die. The Confederates took Colonel Morrow, who fought with the Iron Brigade, from her home as well as a soldier who tried to hide in her chimney a few days ago. When Colonel Morrow observed that soldiers intent, he scolded him and said, "You will not place this family in danger, so come down from there." Well, that lieutenant became very angry and handed Mary a sword and said, "Hide this sword" so I hid it. I asked her if this sword was his. She told me it wasn't and that it belonged to some Confederate general he had captured earlier in the day. She thought he had told her the general's name was Archer. "Wow, a general's sword! No wonder he wanted you to hide it!" I exclaimed. She also added that the lieutenant said he would be back for it, but she is sure he is on his way to Virginia by now. We walked back into the room with the wounded soldiers. Mary brought out some table linens and we began to rip them into bandages. I would scribble down notes in between tasks. Mary caught me doing this out of the corner of her eye and softly said, "Once a reporter, always a reporter." We then searched for pillows and other things we could find to ease the suffering of the wounded.

Just around that time, I noticed the wounded soldier that had been holding the little dog start to cough up blood something terrible, so I propped him up with some books with a pillow on top; it was a crude attempt to ease his suffering, but it was all I could do. He was from the 2nd Wisconsin Infantry and he told me of his two dogs he had back home on his father's farm and how dearly he missed them, as a tear ran down his cheek. Miss McAllister tried to give him some water but he coughed it up too. I feared the end was near for this poor soul. With his eyes half shut and his breathing labored he looked at me and asked, "What name did you decide for the pup?" The dog lay by the soldier's side. I looked at Mary and she looked at me puzzled, then I looked down at one of the books I had used to prop him up and it was the works of Shakespeare. I then looked at the soldier and said, " I named the pup Shakespeare." The young soldier who came all the way from Wisconsin to Gettysburg, Pennsylvania to fight for our Union, looked down at that pup, gently petted his fur and said, "Shakespeare, Shakespeare. I like that," with a small smile emanating from his face. At that moment, his hand dropped to the floor and this brave young man was dead. Miss McAllister and I both had tears in our eyes, as I thought to myself that this poor young man most likely had loved ones back home praying for his safe return which will never come. I was proud to be with him until the end. I am now wondering if finding Shakespeare was not fate but a blessing that the Good Lord planned for us among all the dead and dying that littered the town and fields where these soldiers fought and died these past three days. I also wondered if this rain was in some way God crying for all the carnage before Him and for all the prayers of all the mothers, wives and children offered up to Him for their loved ones safe return home. Or maybe God was just crying for all mankind.

Little Shakespeare

July 5, 1863

I was in such a deep sleep, my whole body relaxed for the first time in days, when I heard laughter coming from the adjoining room. The voices seemed so very familiar that I slowly arose and peered into the next room to find my mother and my wife baking bread. Oh, that mouth-watering fresh baked bread and fresh butter – I can't tell you how so very hungry I am. Please cut me a big piece, I can't wait another second. My mother and wife said nothing, just smiled and began cutting me a big slice and spreading a big clump of that fresh butter on top, but yet not saying a word. How very strange it was, but the smiles on those two women that mean everything to me and seeing them again was more than this reporter could bear. And the fresh baked bread was icing on the cake. Then a loud noise came from outside, of men yelling and running and those two faces I cherish more than anything suddenly turned to fear, as the roar of wagons and yelling became louder. "No no, come back," I yelled as my mother and wife left the room. I was becoming terrified and my heart pounded, "Oh please come back!" Then I awoke; it was all a dream and I was sweating and shaking. I looked around the room as Miss Mary came from the other room and told me I was having a bad dream. A bad dream, I thought to myself, but it was so real. I realized I was still in Gettysburg but it seemed so real until I felt the grumble in my stomach from being so very hungry. Miss Mary handed me a freshly baked piece of bread and how wonderful that piece of bread tasted. I must have dreamed I was safe at home, but I soon realized I was still in Gettysburg.

I peeked out Miss Mary's window to see Union soldiers marching up Chambersburg Street with so many wagons following them; that I could barely hear myself think. Just then I heard a knock at the door. Shakespeare started to bark and I picked him up as Miss Mary and her sister answered the door. Miss Mary greeted the visitor saying, "Hello Mister Wills. How are you? What can I do for you?" "I brought the Colonel over to your house," he said. "He explained that he left something with you days ago and attempted to return but lost his way trying to find your home." Miss Mary looked at me with a puzzled look then she peered outside and loudly exclaimed, "Colonel Morrow, is that you?" She greeted him with a big smile asking," But how? You were taken prisoner!" Miss Mary couldn't contain her curiosity and excitement on how this man could have escaped his captors so quickly. "Hello," said Colonel Morrow, "I have returned for my diary." Miss Mary asked, "In the name of heaven how did you escape?"

I pulled out my pad of paper from my pocket and slowly began to record what I was witnessing. I also shared her excitement on Colonel Morrow's return. He explained he was taken to the college and due to his wound; he was left behind and not taken south, but remained under guard and ordered to tend the wounded, which he did. "They took my sword and coat when they led me away from your home. I was left alone with the wounded for several hours and as it became dark; I put on a surgeon's frock coat and slowly walked toward the back door. Some of the guards were asleep and the two that were awake paid little attention to me as they assumed I was a Confederate surgeon. I prayed they would not pay attention to my blue trousers and they didn't. I basically walked out the back door, thank God. I tried to find your house, but in the darkness I could not do so. I stopped by the home of Mr. Wills and was given refuge in his home. Bless him, I remained there until he said he could escort me and here I am!"

I thought his account was amazing and this would be a great addition to my story; I wrote as fast as I could because this conversation was so utterly fascinating I did not want to leave anything out. Colonel Morrow said that despite losing his sword and coat when taken prisoner, he couldn't leave town without his diary and thanks to Miss Mary's kindness he wouldn't have to. Miss Mary then introduced me and then told him she would retrieve it. Little Shakespeare ran up to the Colonel and jumped up, wagging his tail in excitement. "Well now, I don't seem to remember you," he asked the dog, "were you hiding when I was here?" All three of us chuckled and the Colonel asked if he was mine as he patted Shakespeare on the head. "I guess so, Colonel; I kind of found him in the midst of getting caught in a crossfire under a porch and he has followed me ever since," I explained. Miss Mary walked back to the door with the diary and a sword in her hands. "Here you go Colonel," she said as she handed him the items. The colonel asked whom the sword belonged to. "Confederate General Archer," she said, "don't you remember Dennis Dailey from Wisconsin, Colonel Morrow?" He paused and looked a bit puzzled and then Mary reminded him that Dailey was the man who tried to hide in the chimney. "Of course," said Colonel Morrow, "I remember now." General Archer surrendered the sword to him during the battle. "So Colonel, please promise me if you ever again meet Mister Dailey, you will return the sword to him," Miss Mary said. "I give you my word as an officer and a gentleman," Morrow said. "Thank you for all your kindness," he softly exclaimed as he strapped the sword on and then tipped his hat with a slight bow to Miss Mary. Miss Mary shut the door and was blushing as she smiled at me. I then told her that I should be on my way and thanked her for all the kindness she had shown me, as I walked out the door.

I looked back to see Miss Mary waving and telling me I was always welcome in her home as she walked away humming the tune "Union Forever". "C'mon Shakespeare, let's go," I said. Miss Mary then called out to me, "Don't forget to stop back before you start your journey home and bring your dog." Miss Mary and her sister had taken a liking to

Shakespeare, but I don't believe Mr. Scott was fond of him inside the house. Shakespeare stood next to me wagging his tail as fast as a hummingbird flapping his wings. How innocent he was and so happy despite being in such a horrific place, I thought. I decided to walk to the center of town to see how others had endured the battle. Looking across the street, I spotted two wagons and four men stacking the discarded arms and legs below the window of Christ Lutheran Church. I couldn't believe what I was witnessing. The smell was foul and nauseating and many people put their handkerchief up to their noses and mouths and I thought that if it got any worse I would join them in doing so, as I was starting to become sick myself.

A voice cried out, "Hey Mister!" and I seemed to recognize that voice for it was very familiar, when I turned around I saw my young friend Albertus McCreary with a few friends. "Hello Albertus," I said, "I am so glad to see you well." He started to tell me of his experiences this morning when his attention was distracted. He looked down at Shakespeare and asked, "Is that your dog?" I told him I guess so, just as long as a family in town does not claim him. Albertus then looked at me with a smile and said he was on the battlefield today and they were digging up bodies and putting them in coffins, adding that the smell was so bad it made his stomach sick. He also told me he was on his way to the railroad station with his friends to run an errand for his folks and "pal around" a bit. I thought to myself how easily youth could block out the horror and turn this into an adventure; maybe it was for the best. "Good-bye mister," he said as I waved goodbye and told him to stay out of trouble, which would seem impossibility for young Albertus.

As I continued towards the town "diamond", I could not believe the carnage of this battle all along the street as I looked around. I saw a long line of wagons which appeared to belong to the United States Christian Commission and what a sight it was. The supplies they brought into this war-torn town couldn't have come a moment too soon. The people of town came out to welcome them for their arrival lifted a huge burden off the town in the form of relief for the wounded and hungry. More importantly, it allowed the citizens of this town to be themselves again instead of doctors and nurses whom everyone had become once the wounded started pouring into town due to the fighting. Maybe the town's citizens can get back to their normal lives, but I reluctantly doubted it, for deep down inside I believed they would never be the same again, not even years from now.

I remember arriving here in town, a bright eyed and eager reporter, to visit friends and with the hope of writing a story that might catch the eye of my boss. I remember the tree-lined streets, quiet and untouched by the horrors of war. It was a peaceful, happy town, even after the Confederates left on June 27th. The town felt as if it had made its contributions to this terrible war and would now be passed over by the Confederate Army. Because any additional fighting in town was that of rumor only. But now the reality of war has now hit all those in town like a bolt of lightning. The smell of rotting flesh, corpses bloated to twice their normal size and the dead horses everywhere was indescribable. That and the remnants of an army that occupied the town for three days; with human waste left all about town, attracted the largest swarms of flies. They were everywhere and unfortunately, even on those wounded still laying in the fields. Words could not do the situation justice, nor could a pen express what I see and feel before me in proper terms. The devastation, destruction and death strewn on the streets and fields before me are the most hideous sights my eyes have ever beheld.

In the midst of all these ghastly scenes were people who must have come to town as spectators. And even worse were those who came to pick up souvenirs of the battle and to profit off the dead and dying that fought here protecting them. They are the lowest forms of mankind I've ever seen. Sadly, even some of the residents of town have been observed picking up a gun or knapsack or other articles of the battle. On one hand it saddened me to see these "vultures" swoop in and care only about what they can do to help themselves to a thing or two. On the other hand, it angered me because while they are more interested in lining their pockets, many good men lay in the fields wounded and grasping at life. I am starting to believe that getting the story at any cost may not be the most important part of my life; maybe it is helping the helpless and being the man my mother always wanted me to be. I am beginning to see things a little bit clearer now.

The stench had become so bad in the heat of the afternoon that I began to cough profusely. A man tapped me on the shoulder and asked me to lower my handkerchief from my face. As I did he placed a few drops of some liquid he had in a bottle on the handkerchief. "Is that peppermint?" I asked. "Yes it is," he said, "it is peppermint oil and it seems to make the smell here around town a little easier on the nose and stomach." He introduced himself as David Troxell, who owned a harness and carriage shop. He asked me if I was that reporter who was here to see the Tysons. "Yes, sir," I said, "but how did you know?" He began to tell me how Mrs. Broadhead had hid in his cellar and talked about me, with her daughter Mary telling him about the horse I rode and how grand that horse was. I told him I was wondering if poor old Chester was safe and where the devil he was right now. Mr. Troxell told me some Rebel sharpshooters had been on the roof of his shop and Union artillery shells had seemingly come down in buckets trying to silence them. He then said with a sad look on his face, "I don't believe they hit those Rebs, but they hit some of my carriages in the shop which are now piles of kindling wood." I thanked him again and proceeded down Baltimore Street.

As I walked down the street I still could not fully grasp the destruction of the town and surrounding fields. I remembered what that Confederate soldier told me about the Union Army when they went into Virginia and what they did. One can only imagine what our troops will do after witnessing this battle, if later they go back into Virginia.

While I was walking, pondering the situation here in town, I was lightly slapped on the back. I turned around and there stood two men with pads of paper. They asked, "Hey buddy, were you here during the battle?" "Yes," I said. "What did you see? Did you get hit or anything?" they asked. "No," I said. I started to feel uneasy about these two men; for one thing, they sounded like they might be reporters by the questions they asked. Now, I know a great deal of newspapermen and think of them with great respect, but these two! For one thing they were in fancy, clean clothes and for another thing I witnessed one of them pick up a few things off the ground near the wounded. "Are you fellas from New York?" I asked. "Yep," they said, "sent down here to get the first story from the battle, never expected it to be this bad." The other chimed in "If Lee wanted this dirty town so bad, they should have just given it to him. God knows it stinks to high heaven and we got drenched from the rain yesterday on our way down here!" I looked at these two men and exclaimed, "I am a reporter by trade and I have no respect for two idiots who come to this town when it is now safe and show disrespect to the people of the town and the soldiers who have died or are at this moment dying in those very fields to keep you two pea wits safe. Especially while you waited up north until the battle was over!" "Take it easy buddy," one said. "I will not!" I shouted, "You give us reporters a bad name and to show such disrespect towards this town is a DISGRACE!" As my emotion poured out, Shakespeare, all thirty pounds of puppy, walked to my front, stared at these two men and started to growl. For whatever reason that little dog made me proud.

"All right, all right pal, we'll find someone else to talk to. You're not the only fish in this pond, you know," the first man said. As they started up Baltimore Street, with Shakespeare watching their every move, I yelled out, "Gentlemen, by the way, if I find out you are disrespecting any one of these fine citizens or the wounded I will take you by the scruff of the neck and promise your visit to Gettysburg will be one you will never forget!" As they glanced back at Shakespeare and myself standing our ground, a small group of people and a few soldiers had gathered behind us without my knowing. "You tell them son," an older gentleman spoke out. A few of the soldiers grumbled, "We will remember those two if they bother any of our men."

As the group began to break up, the older gentleman told me his name was Dr. Charles Horner and he appreciated what I had said about the town. "Thank you," I said. To my surprise he then asked, "You say you're a reporter? You wouldn't happen to be that reporter John Burns was going on about, would you?" "Yes, I believe I am, any word on Mr. Burns?" I asked. Dr. Horner told me, "Well, he fought up near the Seminary on the first day of the battle and was hit three times, don't ask me how, but he made it back to his house, a Confederate surgeon attended him." I thought to myself, "He did it, that old man did fight like he said he would and he is a hero." Dr. Horner told me he has been checking in on him and he is recovering nicely. I thanked the doctor for filling me in and asked, "Will you tell Mr. Burns I send him my compliments and in my opinion doctor, that Mr. Burns is one interesting character." As Dr. Horner began walking away he chuckled and said, "Yes, you have that right; he certainly is a character." I had heard the good doctors name around town many times and feel he is well respected, but I thought he seemed to be a different person than when I first took note of him. Maybe there are two Dr. Horner's in town, I wondered.

I continued down Baltimore Street and had many short conversations with people passing by when all of a sudden I gazed down the street and noticed a wagon full of nuns coming up towards me driven by a Catholic priest. I had to look twice, thinking I might need a pair of spectacles. Where in heaven did they come from and how did they get here? I walked toward them, tripping on piles of furniture and everything else the Rebels could find to construct barricades during the fighting. As I approached the wagon I said, "Good day, Father, it's nice to see you." The priest looked down at me and said, "No son, it is not a good day, I am sad to say." I asked if I could be of some assistance to him and the nuns, assuming they were here to help the wounded. "We are on the way to the McClellan Hotel, but you could stop by and help us with the wounded." I said I would do that. He said, "My boy, I am a bit lost; can you tell me where the Catholic Church is located?" He said he had been here in town many times but under much more pleasant days and the streets did not look like this. A voice in the back of the wagon spoke up loudly and said, "Step back and let Father Burlando and the Sisters of St. Joseph's through." I peered around the wagon to see a group of soot covered Union soldiers staring back at me. I jumped back and apologized for holding them up; for some reason it hurt my feelings to know I had caused them a delay in getting to their destination. As I stood there and watched them pass, Father Burlando smiled at me and the nuns in unison said, "Bless you." It made me feel good to see them coming to town, knowing their presence will perk up many a wounded soldier's spirit and help the people of town as well. Heck, they even cheered me up.

It was becoming late in the afternoon now and I decided to make my way toward the McClellan Hotel as I had promised. As I walked back toward the center of town, I could see a group of Confederate soldiers under guard being led down Baltimore Street. As they passed me on my left, each one looked down; they were in the worst condition a human being could be in; dirty, wearing dust covered ragged uniforms and most of them had no shoes, only rags wrapped around their bloody feet. As they moved past me, one of the guards yelled, "Move it you Rebs; you're gonna take the oath or head up north!" All the prisoners were silent and moving almost as if in a trance, but then how else should they look? I guess I would have been in the same depressed way if I were headed south if I had been captured, maybe never able to see my loved ones again. This may sound silly after the past few days, but I actually felt sorry for them. As the last of them were passing me, a large burly man with a face full of long whiskers made eye contact with me. He had the saddest eyes I have ever seen and out of the corner of his eye a tear ran down his cheek. I will never forget this man's face, for back home maybe he was a farmer or a blacksmith, proud to fight for the cause he believed in. Now, with his loved ones a world away and himself reduced to a man broken of body and of spirit, maybe he is wondering if it was all worth it.

As I approached the McClellan Hotel, I noticed the soldiers who had been following the wagon carrying Father Burlando and the Sisters were now unloading the wagon. Rather then annoying them with my presence, I decided to steer clear of them since some of them were good-sized men. I decided to head over to my friend Charles' photography studio. Maybe by now he has returned with Chester. Shakespeare and I peeked into the studio windows and realized Charles had not yet returned, but I was able to procure some bread and an apple from some people with the Sanitary Commission. I found a nice shaded spot and decided to take a rest with Shakespeare; we ate the bread and that had to be the finest apple I have ever eaten and I know Shakespeare enjoyed his portion of our bounty of food. The next thing I knew we had both fallen asleep.

We must have been sleeping for an hour or so when we heard more wagons coming into town. We awoke to hear screaming coming from up the street out of the open windows of the houses that were serving as hospitals. I continued further up York Street where a small group of people were gathered in a circle-like group at the corner of Stratton Street. As I walked over, it appeared they were looking at the body of a Union soldier, but there were a lot of dead soldiers, so why was he so unique? As I got closer, I was amazed to see the body of a man grasping an ambrotype photograph of three children. A young girl bent over and pried the picture from the dead man's grasp as each one of us thought of this poor soldier's final moments when he was taking his last breath and found comfort gazing at his three children before life would leave his body. The girl told me she was going to give the picture to her father, whose name was Benjamin Shriver and owned a local tavern. I wonder if I will ever find out the names of these children.

I have seen many horrible things since I have been in Gettysburg and many touching things as well. I will never forget that picture of those three children of the battlefield as I will call them, most likely praying for their father's safe return home, but they will never see him again. He will never see his children grow up and they will never feel his touch or hear his voice again. How very sad that is. We continued walking around observing all the carnage this town endured. We also helped any of the remaining wounded into the field hospitals in that area of town.

It is now late and I badly wanted to return home, but will stay here until Charles and Maria return and I pray that Chester will return as well. As for Shakespeare and myself, I think we will call it a night. I am not much for sleeping outdoors but tonight I would prefer to sleep under the stars. If only that smell would go away...

July 6, 1863

As I awoke, I decided to honor my promise to the Sisters, so Shakespeare and I headed to the McClellan Hotel. I entered the hotel to the sound of a screaming man who was being operated on by two surgeons and three other men holding him down, behind a thin piece of cloth, which was used as a divider or wall. The other side of the wall was where the wounded were being tended by the Sisters. One of the Sisters who came up from Emmitsburg was tending to the wounded and was gently dressing their wounds while at the same time praying. Shakespeare who has never left my side was terrified of the screams as he trembled in my arms. I will never be able to do this moment justice by just writing about it, as one has to experience this to realize just how terrible war is. The flies seem to invade Gettysburg, feasting on the dead and dying and the smell - oh, the smell - was most putrid. Yesterday, the town spread chloride of lime on the streets to disinfect the mud, manure and puddles around town. I really don't know if it helped because the smell of disinfectant mixed with the other odors really seemed to make it more unpleasant. The smell from the streets came inside through the window and I know when I go outside it will be far worse but in some strange way some of the citizens and myself have become acclimated to it. Yesterday as I walked around town, I was hungry and I know little Shakespeare was as well and I had found very little to eat, so today I will venture out to see if I can find some food. I wouldn't dare ask for food here in this hospital for my pride would not allow me when so many men are dying around me and are in much greater need. I heard a rumor that some trains may be stopping close to town with much needed supplies; maybe they can spare some food for Shakespeare and myself.

All of a sudden I realized there was silence from the man behind that makeshift room - no more screams, only silence. As two stretcher-bearers removed him, one of the surgeons came out and sat on the floor next to me. He was covered in blood and sweat was pouring down his face. After wiping his brow, he turned to me and said, "I can't take much more of this." He told me he was at it all night and he wonders if the wounded being brought into these makeshift hospitals would ever end. "We are running low on supplies," he said, "and the flies are everywhere." He also said he has cut off more arms and legs during these last few days than a regular surgeon does in a lifetime. "That last man we tried to save died right there on the table after we removed the lower half of both legs," he lamented. He added that, "I have not an ounce of strength left in this body after operating for ten hours straight, I need some rest and"...........This poor man fell asleep before he could finish his sentence.

I couldn't imagine all the horrors this exhausted man had to endure and to fall asleep so quickly upon sitting down only shows how utterly tired he was. I thought to myself how horrible it was for me on July 2nd when I was in the Catholic Church and now it was unfolding before my eyes again. I did not want to experience it again; cowardly of me perhaps, but it disturbed me mentally not being able to help these poor souls on the surgeon's table. I am just not strong enough. Then a voice of the surgeon yelled out, " Hey you! Come over here, we need you!" I hesitated, frozen in fear. "Move it," he said, "we need you to hold this man down." What could I do? I slowly moved toward that table behind the curtain. On the table, a most gruesome sight waited; a man was lying there, his leg dangling. He was barely able to open his eyes. The surgeon probed a bullet wound with his finger in the man's arm as the he moaned in pain. The soldier had been struck in at least three places in his arm. Then, as the surgeon removed two minie balls from his wounds, the man moaned in pain. As he probed the third wound, maggots began to pour out of it. A more ghastly sight I have never beheld. The stench was so great; that I was becoming sick to my stomach. Then the surgeon pulled out his saw and began sawing through the man's leg, apparently the result of an artillery wound. It was July 2nd all over again for me, but this time I remained determined to make up for my actions on July 2nd and stay with the wounded. The man who was in such excruciating pain stared back at me as I and two other men held him down. It was soon over. The amputated leg of this man was heaped onto a pile of other limbs outside the window like a pile of cordwood. Another man was quickly laid on the table as the man with one leg was removed to where the other wounded were being tended to by the Sisters from Emmitsburg.

The next man did not fare much better. His hand was nothing more than a bloody stump with four of his fingers missing. He had also been hit by artillery fire and I cannot understand how he only lost part of a hand. The man said he was from New York City. He had been lying out in the field for days and was finally tended to by one of the farmers on July 4th. He was part of the 45th New York Infantry and I had trouble understanding his heavy German accent. He was very weak due to the loss of blood and said that his best friend was blown to pieces by the artillery round that hit him. I realized that this man was covered in the blood of his friend, more so than of his own. As we held this man down, what looked like a horn of a bull was placed over his face. As the surgeon dripped something into it, the man began to go into a deep sleep. The surgeon told me to, "Let go, he ain't going nowhere now." I asked him why he didn't do that for the last man. He answered, "Because I don't have a lot of the chloroform left and this man has a better chance to live after I take his hand off." I now felt badly for the first man. I could still hear him moaning in pain on the other side of the curtain. "You can let go now," the surgeon said, "we are gong to take a rest now." I looked down and noticed I was standing in a pool of blood. How many men must have been on this table and how many more men will soon be brought here after I leave, I wondered.

As I left the bloody table area, I went back to where I noticed the first surgeon was still sleeping where I had left him. A Sister tapped me on the shoulder and asked, "Young man, would you so kind as to assist me? I have to get back to the Methodist Church and I have these supplies I must deliver." "It will be my pleasure, Sister," I said. I so wanted to leave this place and this was a good excuse, but I also wanted to help the Sisters, these "Angels of the Battlefield" in any way I could. The Sister then turned to me and said, "Your dog has been waiting for you." I told her he hadn't left me since I found him. "You found him?" she asked. "Yes," I answered, "he and I have been through a lot together these past few days and I guess I am the only family he has. I guess he is pretty lucky." "Oh no, my son," she said, "luck has nothing to do with it, maybe God decided you needed him as much as he needed you." I thought about what she had said and realized she was absolutely correct. "You are right Sister; this little puppy not only brought a smile to my face but also to some of the wounded as well." She then said, "God's angels come in many different forms my son." "Thank you Sister," I said, "I really needed that and you are right; this puppy, I mean Shakespeare, has been a blessing. Now what do you need me to do?" "May I ask your name Sister," I asked her, as she deserved that respect. "I am Sister Camilla and I need to pick up more supplies from the army commissaries in town; will you help distribute them, my son?" I said, "Sister, you can depend on me to help you the best I can." She looked at me and smiled, then waved me to follow her as we left the hotel.

As we walked outside I whispered under my breath, "Oh my!" The stench was absolutely nauseating. I put the hand-kerchief back up to my mouth and nose but Sister Camilla just walked ahead without even covering her nose. She didn't seem affected by the odor but was a bit upset at the sights around town. We entered the commissaries' office and a heavy-set man in uniform; I believe he was a Sergeant, asked, "Well, Sister, in need of supplies at the Catholic Church?" Sister Camilla looked at the sergeant and said, "I will later, but for now they should go to the Methodist Church Hospital since they are in the most need." I think the Sergeant was caught off guard by the fact that she, a Catholic nun, would be in a church of a different denomination. Just then another Sister walked up to us and asked, "Were you able to procure the supplies needed for the Methodist Church Hospital?" "Yes, Reverend Mother, this kind man has granted our request and is gathering supplies." The Sergeant turned around and smiled at them and said, "You Sisters are a blessing to the wounded, both Union and Confederate; you need only ask and I will help you as best that I can." I wondered who this other Sister was as she seemed to be the one who was in charge. Sister Camilla turned to me and said, "I am sorry, this is Mother Ann Simeon Norris of St. Joseph's in Emmitsburg." "You are helping too? Bless you, my son," said Mother Ann Simeon. "You are more than welcome Mother," I said. I had a hold of a large wooden box filled with all kinds of bandages and other items for the wounded. Mother Ann looked down at Shakespeare and said, "Oh, we seem to have a new friend." Sister Camilla spoke up and said, "Reverend Mother, that is Shakespeare and he is this kind man's little dog. They just met and the dog has not left his side." "Shakespeare, hmmm, what a clever name for a dog," she said with a smile as we started to walk. Shakespeare followed behind wagging his tail.

Walking down the street with the Sisters I felt as if I was walking with royalty. Most citizens would stop to look and most would say, "Good afternoon Sisters" or "It's nice to see you in town!" as we continued on our way. That large kindhearted lady who hugged me on the steps of the church before the battle, started toward us in a quick walk and excitedly started talking with the Sisters. I must admit that the wooden box was becoming very heavy and although I was still able to carry it, I was really starting to feel the effects of sleeping on hard floors for the past five nights and I would have given my left arm for a hot bath. I suddenly realized that many had given their left arms and more for our country and even though I had been exaggerating in my thoughts, I felt shame for thinking it, what with all the death around me. But the fact remained, that I needed a bath and I am sure if my wife were here she would strongly agree. We turned onto Middle Street, to the Methodist Church and when we went inside I could hear men moaning in pain. "Put that box down right here," one Sister told me, as another Sister and an orderly came over to the box and started to remove its contents. The orderly said, "Supplies, oh thank goodness, how we can use them!" A nice older woman came in with some fresh bread and started to hand it out. She handed me a piece and told me I must be hungry from carrying that box. "Oh yes, thank you," I said. She asked me if that dog belonged to me and I said, "Yes, he does, why do you ask?" "Well, I made some broth for the wounded and if you would help me distribute it to the wounded, I will let your dog have the soup bone I used to make the broth." I agreed and she pulled the bone out of a large pot that she carried and I gave it to Shakespeare. He took that bone and walked to the front door with it and he sat next to a guard at the front of the church as I followed. "I'll watch him for you, mister, but I can't leave my post," said the guard. Shakespeare lay down beside him and excitedly started chewing on the bone. I walked back inside and Sister Camilla ran over to me and said, "There you are. I had hoped you didn't leave without me thanking you." "No Sister, I am going to help this nice lady hand out her bread and broth she brought." I pointed out Shakespeare chomping on that soup bone and Sister Camilla looked at this kind woman and said, "Oh bless you for your kindness." The woman replied "Oh no Sister, thank you for coming to this town and helping." Bless you and everyone who has come here to help." She patted me on the shoulder and smiled.

The wounded in this hospital were fewer in number compared to the Catholic Church and it was not as hectic and disorganized, as the Catholic Church. We gave bread to all those who could eat by themselves and the broth was put into several bowls and spoon fed by the Sisters to those who could not feed themselves. As we were passing out bread, I noticed a man dressed in black kneeling over a badly wounded man; it looked like he might be a minister of some sort who was baptizing the man. The wounded man looked at Sister Camilla and asked, "Is he doing it the right way Sister, like they say in the bible?" as she smiled and nodded yes to indicate he was doing it correctly. The Sister then knelt beside the man and they both began to pray. The man was gasping for air due to his wound and yelled out with every ounce of strength he had left, "God bless these good Sisters!" Then the gasping for air stopped and the man was dead. Sister Camilla prayed over him and soon moved on to another wounded man. She was saddened by what had just occurred but realized others still needed her help. The men were so very grateful, Union and Confederate alike. One young soldier looked up toward one of the Sisters who was tenderly feeding him as if his mother or grandmother were feeding him. He had bright blue eyes and blond hair and was wearing a Confederate uniform. I truly believe God in heaven has heard the prayers of a mother or grandmother in some southern town for the safe return of this young man who is so far from home. Maybe the Sisters were a sign from God that kindness and goodness still exist in these times of death and destruction. Maybe through the Sisters and volunteers who have come to Gettysburg, who have shown that good is greater than evil, that kindness towards one's fellow man still exists and if only we as a country would have seen this years ago, then this war would never have started.

I felt a pull of my trousers and looked down - a wounded soldier who looked to be around thirty had his right arm amputated just below the elbow. He asked, "Can you write a letter to my wife and children?" I said, "I sure can," and proceeded to write as he spoke. He said, "My dear wife, I lay here in Gettysburg, Pennsylvania in a church with about thirty other wounded men, some far worse off than me. I was wounded in a battle at a brickyard when my regiment was flanked and we began to run through town. I was shot twice in the arm and they removed it from the elbow down." His eyes began to tear up and his voice cracked with sadness, then he continued. "Oh, how I miss that beautiful smile of yours and the laughter of the children playing. Oh, my dear, I so badly wish to see you again for I am in such pain and hope it will not be my last days. I want to tell you I love you and I love our dear young ones so much that if I get home then I will never go off again. I will never leave you no matter if a hundred wars start. And my dear wife, if I do return even missing part of my arm, I will be twice the man I was before I left, for the horrors of war changed me after seeing men die like my dear friend Amos, who was shot next to me as we ran. I have seen such horrors during this war, men slaughtering each other. You know that I was not a believer but I now know I was wrong for when I began this battle I knew if a merciful God existed he would not allow all these terrible things to happen and it confirmed my stance on the subject when I arrived here. When these Sisters came to this church and helped and showed compassion towards Union and Confederate alike and treated us like "children of God", as they put it, I now know that you were right and God is real. I promise if I come home I will go to service with you and the children each and every Sunday, for my dear, I was so very wrong and I want to say I am sorry for the disagreements we have had on the subject. I love you, Robert."

I comforted him as he wiped the tears away from his face with his uninjured arm. Then he looked at me and said, "Mister, do you believe in God?" I looked down and said, "Yes, more now during these last six days than ever before." He told me he wanted to change his ways and prove to his wife that he truly was serious about God and becoming the husband and father he had never been before. I thought about it and told him I could help. He looked at me with a puzzled expression. I walked over to Sister Camilla and whispered to her. She walked over to the wounded soldier and asked, ""Would you like to be baptized, my son?" "Oh dear sister, more than you know," he said. I figured I would leave as not to embarrass him, when once again he grabbed my trousers and said, "Thank you, oh, thank you so much. If ever I get home, I hope we will meet again so I can show you my family." I looked back at him and said, "I wish the same and hope you get well quickly and return to your family." As I walked away, about three other men not badly wounded nodded to me and said, "Thank you," to which I added, "get well soon men."

It was a very sad sight to see so many wounded men, some very bad off. A farmer brought in fresh straw to place under some of the wounded and I decided to offer my help. "Excuse me sir, I can help you with that," I said. I grabbed a large bundle of straw and walked toward a young soldier who I believe was a Confederate. This poor soul had his eyes bandaged as well as having both legs amputated at the knees. I decided to put some straw under him, "There my good lad is that better," I asked him. He turned to me unable to see me but said, "Thank ya kindly sir." I asked him if there is anything else I could do for him when he said in a crackling voice, "Take me home." I stared at him and asked where is home, he told me he was from Georgia and he lost his brother when a artillery shell exploded next to them. I thought to myself knowing this poor boy was not long for this world but maybe I could talk to him and bring some sort of comfort to him, I couldn't just leave him. "Mister, ya know I'm a Confederate soldier in this here town and I can't believe the people here have been so kind to me," he said. I looked at him and said I see no enemy, only a young man like myself who is a stranger in this town"

"You mister, you're a stranger in these parts?" he said. "Yes, I am from Pennsylvania but miles away from Gettysburg." He was struggling in his words, his breathing was becoming labored. He said, "Mister, I want to go home to my family and farm. I have two wee little sisters who I fear I will not be with again, nor can I run for my legs are gone," he said. I told him to stay strong in spirit and maybe by the grace of the Good Lord he will get better. He said "Will ya say a prayer for me?" he then told me of the large farm he lived on in Georgia and how he wished to return there to his mother and sisters.

He added, " I would run and run with my dog after my chores were done to my favorite fishin' hole and just stare up at the birds wishing I were one of em. I wanted ta fly away from Georgia with em and see the world and explore it all, but now I recon I would give anything to fly back home with em, to that fishin hole and be with my mother and sisters and run like the blazes with my dog...............Mister, I wanna go home."

I stood there in silence, if only that brave young man could see the tears streaming down my face. I composed myself and said "You will get home my friend." The boy smiled and I then told him, "I will return before I leave and check up on you." The wounded Confederate just shook his head and extended his hand to me, we shook hands and I went on to help the Sisters. Later that day I found out that Confederate soldier had died of his wounds, it affected me so deeply because I so wanted this man to live.

I heard Shakespeare outside barking but it was not his normal bark, something was wrong! I ran outside and who do you think I saw but those two New York reporters disturbing that nice old lady who gave Shakespeare that soup bone. She backed away from them and I heard them ask, "Can't ya tell us why you came here old woman and are there any Rebels among the wounded in there?" Shakespeare was showing his teeth as he stood between the old woman and those two vultures. I shouted, "Hey what did I tell you about bothering the wounded?" "Oh it's you again, well ya better get that mutt away from us or he will find my foot along side his head!" one of them said. As I stood in the doorway, a group of soldiers were drinking coffee and overheard the commotion. I thought to myself about all the good I had seen from people, but I realize the bad when I see it and these two were rotten to the core! I started to run toward them when that group of soldiers beat me to it. I ran over, grabbed Shakespeare and said, "Gentlemen, these two have been bothering the volunteers as you have just witnessed." One of the two men said, "Hey we're just doing our job." That's when I interrupted him and said, "I am a REPORTER too and I would much rather aid the wounded than be a nuisance to them."

One large soldier, Irish I believe by his accent, spoke up and said, "Nuisance, ya say boyo, well I tink you lads better come widt us." "Hey wait," those two said as they pointed back to me and added, "That guy and his mangy dog are the ones bothering us." The soldier stood silent and shook his head, looked at them with an angry look and said, "dis man here and his wee little dog helped the good Sisters by bringing supplies and helped this wonderful woman feed the wounded," as he pointed to the nice lady that gave Shakespeare the bone and boiling coffee, apparently the same coffee these soldiers were drinking. "Now boyo, ya better come with us and leave these good people alone and we here would like ta have a talk with you two fine men." These two reporters who I hate to even call reporters walked away with that group of soldiers, sarcastic fear on their faces, when the big Irish soldier turned his head and winked at me with a big smile. Needless to say, I am sure they were escorted to the city limits after being taught a lesson. I was just glad to never see them again. "Good boy, Shakespeare," I said, as that nice old lady looked at me and said, "My name is Martha and I came from Hanover to help." She knelt down and patted Shakespeare on the head and said, "Thank you Shakespeare, you brave little dog for looking after me." I thanked her for her kindness and we were on our way.

We walked up High Street to Washington Street, then up Chambersburg Street past the porch where I had hid and met Shakespeare on the fourth day and continued toward the Seminary. Then I realized I didn't have my handkerchief over my nose as I stared at the carnage in the fields. I saw two things that greatly disturbed me. Union soldiers were lining up the dead for burial, many of the Confederate soldiers were scattered over the field, some still moving. Of the dead, many had their pockets cut out, most likely by the human "filth" that came to rob the dead. And there were piles of dead horses being burned. It made me think of my horse Chester and wonder if he was still alive. I am not ashamed to say that tears formed in my eyes thinking about him. Soldiers were also picking up muskets and many civilians were helping, but none that I had ever seen before in town. The mud was thick in some parts of the road, but since I wasn't looking down, I stepped knee-deep in a puddle. Goodness, I thought to myself, as I took off my shoe and shook the mud out. Two soldiers yelled out, "Halt" and approached me. I sat there when they came up to me and said, "What are you doing? Get in line with the rest of them!" I looked at them confused and said, "I was going up toward the Seminary when I stepped in this puddle and I wasn't doing anything wrong." They looked at each other and told me to move along. I asked who these people were who were picking up equipment and digging graves. I was told that they were robbers and thieves who had come to rob the dead. "So you make them dig graves?" I asked. "That's right, we'll teach them what happens when thieves steal from our dead and wounded. Now move along!" he shouted. "I am sorry, I meant no disrespect and I just can't believe someone could steal from a deceased man, it's horrible!" I said. I continued to walk up the street until I was close to the Seminary grounds, the sun was setting and it was getting darker by the minute.

On the way up the road I noticed an unexploded artillery shell lodged in the front of a house. I wondered if the family owning the house is even aware that it's there, before the battle I was told it was some sort of school. I then noticed a group of Confederate prisoners who were under guard and most likely part of the grave digging detail, resting on what appeared to be barricades left from the battle. Some of them were asleep, some standing and all were very tired and exhausted. I asked one of them where they were from and they answered that they were from Alabama and North Carolina. The guard standing next to these men told me to keep moving and I'm not allowed to talk to them. I took the hint and decided it was in my best interest to continue on my way and not irritate anyone holding a rifle. Moving onto the Seminary grounds, I beheld total devastation. It was hard to believe this was the same area I visited on the 30th of June. The trees, many destroyed and riddled with bullets, looked as if a tornado had come through the area, bodies of many horses littered the grounds. Many of the dead soldiers were so swollen that they no longer could be identified, their faces black from facing the sun. The horses were being pulled with ropes into piles and were then burned. What I thought was very strange was the fact that a man and a young boy, possibly his son, picking up unexploded artillery shells. "Are they CRAZY!" I thought they could be killed if one of those artillery rounds would go off. I yelled at them from a distance, "Hey, what are you doing? Leave those alone, do you want to be killed?" The man and the boy waved me off saying, "The Army is paying thirteen cents a pound for this metal, go find your own and leave us be!" How could this man possibly sacrifice the life of his boy and himself for thirteen cents a pound? I have to admit; that I think some people have no common sense at all doing such things, but either way, I plan to keep my distance from those two.

I realized I needed to find somewhere to sleep tonight. My body was very sore and stiff from sleeping arrangements these last few nights and I thought that maybe tonight I would sleep under a tree and upon some soft grass, where the air was more tolerable. I was sure it couldn't be any worse than those hard floors, as long as it didn't rain tonight.

As I found a tree on the grounds of the Seminary, a man not far from me in a wagon, walked over to me. I thought to myself, "What now?" Hopefully he doesn't have any artillery rounds with him for thirteen cents a pound! "Hello there," he said. Cautiously, I said, "Hello." "I am a photographer and I am boiling coffee. Would you like some?" he asked. "Why yes, thank you," I said and felt guilty about judging him as he had walked over. He invited me to where he was boiling coffee and something on that fire smelled good. We talked about our professions and he asked me about some of the scenes I had encountered around town over a plate of rice and beans. Shakespeare polished off his dinner and was soon sound asleep. He told me of the many pictures he took in the surrounding fields of the dead and we both agreed the aftermath of the battle was awful with such ghastly sights we have never beheld before. It was now getting late and I thanked him for his hospitality. He even said he will be returning home up north in a few days and if I needed a ride he would welcome the company. He was a very nice man to converse with and I was thankful of his offer of a ride but I must leave tomorrow.

Stretching out under the stars and with Shakespeare besides me, it was now time for me to get some sleep. Tomorrow I am heading home.

Confederate prisoners near the Seminary.
Library of Congress

July 7, 1863

Waking up, my clothes were wet with the morning dew, but I had enjoyed a deep relaxing night's sleep. This will have to be the day I return home. I so badly want to go home but doing so without Chester will take an eternity on foot, but most importantly I will have lost a member of our family. That horse meant the world to my wife. I looked around under full sunlight, I could see so much more than I did yesterday. I could see arms and legs protruding from the ground, no doubt from hastily dug graves marked with crude headboards made of ammunition crates and anything else that could be obtained. I could see an older woman wearing tattered clothes walking back and forth with baskets to the farm further up the Chambersburg Pike. I heard a familiar voice yell out, "Hello!" and as I turned I saw it was Mrs. Broadhead carrying baskets of food towards the Seminary. "I am glad to see you again," she said. "As I am to see you," I said. "Where is little Mary?" "Oh," she said, "with this horrible smell I decided it was best for her to stay at home with Joseph. I was here yesterday helping the wounded and it was truly a horrible sight seeing these poor men in such horrible conditions. I brought some baked goods from the women in town and I will give it to the wounded." I asked about that woman walking toward that farm with the torn clothing. She said it was Sarah Foulk and pointed to a house that showed the effects of the battle. It had been struck many times and I guess that is why the woman's clothes were full of holes. "Does she live there?" I asked. "No, that's her mother's, the widow Thompson's house and it is said her house and surrounding land was the camp of Confederate General Robert E. Lee and stayed there in her house during the battle," she told me. "Sarah has been delivering bread to the wounded everyday even during the battle, bless her soul," Mrs. Broadhead added, "and now I have to deliver these baskets." "Please let me help you carry those baskets," I said. She whispered, "Would you like some bread or have you already eaten?" I told her I haven't and she pulled out a piece of fresh bread and gave it to me. "Thank you," I said as we headed back toward the Seminary. The scene inside was just as horrible as the smell outside. Discarded arms and legs littered the grounds, thrown out a window I assumed. Men and women aiding the wounded, running back and forth, I can hear the moans of pain coming from all those poor souls inside. I dropped off the baskets with an orderly and Mrs. Broadhead thanked me. The air inside was putrid and stale and it was so terribly hot inside. I could not imagine being wounded and lying in such a place, but where else can they go? Mrs. Broadhead went up to the second floor and I decided to head back to town. I felt guilty leaving but if I am going to leave town, then I must try to get supplies as soon as possible.

The amount of people seemed to have tripled, as well as more wagons most likely to aid the wounded and more curious people, many with good intentions, I'm sure. I was almost to town when I heard a voice I had so wanted to hear yell out, "Hey young fella!"

I turned and who should I see but Old Man Burns sitting on his porch with bandages covering his wounds. "I got a good story for your paper," he said. I nodded and said, "I am sure you do." "I left ya that day and moved up the pike. The first bunch of soldiers made me move along, they didn't believe I could fight. I found a regiment and stood side by side with 'em and showed those Rebs a thing or two just like I told ya, but then I was hit. Henry eventually brought me back to my house. I must have killed ten or twenty of those Rebs and if they come back I'll show em again!" I remembered what those Confederates had said about that bushwhacker on the ridge, so I asked him why he had not been taken prisoner. "I fought the British years ago and they couldn't take me and if those Rebs think they can take me, they got another thing comin!" He hesitated and said that they knew the better of it. " You let them know in your paper that if they want a fight and come back to Gettysburg, John Burns is awaitin!" Mrs. Burns brought John a bowl of some sort of stew out to him. As she left us, she looked at me and rolled her eyes and smiled.

Mr. Burns was furious about the fact that no other men in town had taken up arms with him and he was not shy about naming them. Even Mr. Broadhead was mentioned among many others that he considered cowards. Mister Burns then asked me, "And where were you young fella when the shootin started?" What could I say without having him criticize me? I thought about it and said, "Well, Mr. Burns, being a stranger, I became lost and caught up in the confusion of it all, but I have to compliment you for your courage that you exhibited for your town and country, you are a hero." "So tell me about the battle?" I said. "Well like I told ya," he continued, "I killed forty of those Rebs before I was shot and I wasn't gonna let those Rebs take me away. They wanted to take me prisoner, but I guess they thought the better of it after I put up a fight." "I am the damn constable ya know and I'd lock up that General Lee of theirs if he was about town, but I never saw him," he said. I thought to myself that this was one tough old rooster; he actually did fight and was wounded so I do have a lot of respect for him. He again looked me in the eye and started to tell me about one Confederate that got about five feet from him until he shot him. But in mid-sentence, he stopped talking and looked down at the bowl of stew in silence. I was about to ask him if he was allright until he looked up and said, "Dang it, I told her not to put so much pepper in my stew." This was meant, I believe, for Mrs. Burns. It struck me as being funny. Now composed, he said, "There were a few fellas who were reporters in town and they wanted to talk to me but I think they wanted to sell me something so I told them to git. Anyways, that's about all I got to tell ya, so make sure you spell my name right when you're writin that article about me." I assured him all is in order and I will submit my story to my paper as soon as I return home. I got the impression that Mr. Burns thought my entire story would be about him. I knew better but thanked him for his time and told him his courage inspired me, which it did.

John Burns
Courtesy of the Adams County Historical Society

As I left Mister Burns, I figured I would stop by Miss Mary's house and the McCreary home as well as Professor Jacobs and thank them for all they did for me. Then I needed to round up those supplies and make that long journey home. I started to walk down Chambersburg Street when I saw that a wagon had lost a wheel and a crowd of people was gathered around it trying to fix it. "Great," I said, realizing that huge crowd of people are right in front of my friends Charles'and Maria's home. I'll walk down Middle Street and thank the professor first. I turned down Middle Street hoping to bypass all the crowds; they have swollen to four times the size during the night. It was much more crowded and I didn't want Shakespeare getting lost or God forbid, hurt by some careless wagon driver. As I walked down the street, it looked like Professor Jacobs was in the distance. As I moved closer, I could see he was talking to a man in a gray uniform. As crazy as it seemed Professor Jacobs was talking to a Confederate soldier! Did he capture him? Or was he hiding somewhere? I called out, "Professor, it's me, is everything all right?" "Oh, quite all right, he said, May I introduce you to one of my former pupils, James Crocker?" I stood with what must have seemed a very blank look on my face. What was the good professor doing talking to the enemy in the side open? I would assume many in town would not find favor in this act. I introduced myself and said, "Were you involved in any of the fighting around town?" He looked at me and said, "Why yes, I served in General Pickett's division and on July 3rd we marched toward a stone wall that thousands of Union soldiers were hiding behind." He started to tell me how many of his division were cut down and some made it past the wall and it would be the last time he saw General Armistead, who regrettably would die days later. He appeared to become very emotional when he told me about General Armistead and said he had been one of the South's best and most compassionate generals and will be missed. Oh, how odd it was to be talking to a soldier from the invading army but this man seemed to be more a part of Gettysburg than the Confederate Army. I thanked the Professor for his kindness during my stay in Gettysburg and said I hoped to return in the Fall if possible. I also shook James Crocker's hand and wished him well. Just then my little friend Charles McCurdy was running by, but stopped to look at James Crocker. I said, "Charles, it's nice to see you again." Staring at James Crocker in awe, he told me, "We have a Confederate general staying at our house." Crocker asked, "Which general, my good lad, is staying with you? "General Trimble," he answered, "and he told me stories and gave me a nice pocketknife." Professor Jacobs looked at Charles and said, "Not too loud my boy, some people might not take kindly to your family caring for a Confederate general in your house." Charles looked at James Crocker and said, "What about him, you're talking to him and nobody seems to mind?" I looked at the Professor as did James Crocker and said, "He has a good point." The Professor laughed and said, "Charles, I so look forward to seeing you in one of my classes in the future. But what if Mister Burns were to find this out about the general, what then?" Charles looked in the direction of John Burns house and said, "Ya think he'd lock me up?"

We all laughed and the Professor said, "Let's not take a chance," as he warned Crocker about venturing towards John Burns' house. James Crocker laughed and said, "Some things in this town never change." As I walked away, I wrote down what I had just witnessed that a former resident of town would be a part of the Confederate Army and be allowed to roam the town because even I would have trouble explaining it later. I thought to myself, if I were to actually leave today it would have to be in the next two hours because I want to get as far as I can before nightfall. I walked towards Charles photography studio via High street. "Oh hello Miss

Myers, how are you?" I greeted her as I approached. "Is Sergeant Stewart still staying with you?" She looked toward the ground; I had no doubt brought up a sensitive subject. She looked up and told me, "Sergeant Stewart died. He died in my house. He was so brave even until the very end of his life." I could see the tears rolling down her cheek. I had never felt like such an insensitive cad before. I never wanted to cause this brave young woman any more pain. I said, "May God bless you Miss Myers, for providing comfort to these soldiers in their last hours of life in this terrible war." I did feel badly. She said, "Thank you for all that you said and you're right, this is a terrible war when men can kill one another and will continue to kill one another." She also told me she has learned so much about herself, about how the need to help ones fellow man no matter how gruesome the situation may be. She said she is going to continue to nurse the wounded until they are all moved from Gettysburg. I told her, "Miss Myers, I will never forget you and it is an honor to have made your acquaintance." She wished me well and I continued up High Street to Baltimore Street, when I suddenly noticed the amount of people in the "Diamond."

It seems like everyone is coming to Gettysburg. I only hope they have good intentions and do not take advantage of the sufferings of others. A wagon passed me with a driver and two women weeping with what appeared to be a wooden casket in the back. I can't imagine the sadness in these two women. They could have been a mother, sister or wife. They came to Gettysburg to find a loved one, no doubt hoping to find him safe but they now return home with only a body of the fallen loved one they came to find. It is very sad, very sad indeed.

As I approached the Photography Studio, I noticed it was still empty inside. My friend Charles had not returned. I fear my friends and Chester may have met an undesired situation and may have been captured and sent down South. I feel I have no choice but to head home alone with Shakespeare for my work here is finished, except for the fate of my dear friends and horse. I promised Miss Mary I would say goodbye and I would make good on that promise so I headed down Chambersburg Street. "Stay close Shakespeare, I don't want to lose you like the others," I told my four-legged companion. "My goodness, the congestion on this street is horrible. Where are all these people coming from? It seems like it could take an hour just to get to Miss Mary's house," I said aloud as I tried to weave through the congestion on the street. I heard the sounds of horses that were most likely getting impatient of the logjam in the middle of the road. I picked up Shakespeare and decided to get off Chambersburg Street and take one of the alleys. Then I heard the cry of a horse...I would swear that sounds like...CHESTER and riding him was CHARLES! They rode toward me through the crowd as I ran toward them. I am not ashamed to say the tears were flowing down my cheeks with joy when Charles and I said at the same exact moment, "Where have you been?" and again we responded out at the same moment "looking for you!" I put Shakespeare down and grabbed the reins of Chester and exclaimed, "There's my good horse," as I patted his head. Charles jumped off and embraced me. After the last seven days this was the finest moment of them all. I asked, "Where is Maria?" "Oh, quite safe," Charles said, "she is at home cleaning. Surprisingly they took very little, but started a fire on our carpet and other than those Rebs taking my clothing, the house suffered little damage. An artillery shell is lodged in the front of my studio and did some damage but nothing was taken, thank God it did not explode or the damage would have been extensive...but where in heavens have you been?" I told him all I had been through as we walked back to his home. Little Shakespeare started to bark when Charles asked "And who is this?" I told him all about Shakespeare and as we approached the front door Maria came running out and Charles exclaimed, "Look who I found!" Maria yelled out my name "ROBERT!" as she hugged me. "Thank God, we were so afraid we had lost you when we came back to town on July 5th and couldn't find you." "On the fifth?" I exclaimed, "Do you mean to tell me you have been in town for two days?" as I looked in amazement at my two friends. They turned to each other, shrugged their shoulders and said, "Why, yes we have." I didn't have the words as we looked at one another and then broke into laughter. Maria told me that a barrel of flour in the pantry was right where they left it even after Confederates had been through the house and she was going to be baking some bread very soon. I told her I was planning on leaving for home so I could only stay for a short while. Besides, I thought, fresh bread was just what the doctor ordered. I would also have the pleasure of washing up for the first time in all these days. "One cannot always appreciate this simple act which we take for granted." Afterwards, I felt refreshed physically and in some ways mentally as well. Charles had a few shirts that he had taken with him when he left town. He offered me one; we were close to the same size. I told him how much I appreciated it, especially since he only had about four shirts left to his name. The Confederates took the clothes in the house and left their rags in its place, no doubt some covered with lice. Charles had disposed of them immediately.

After spending time with my friends sharing our experiences of the battle, I sadly told them it was soon time for us to leave. I told Maria I would be back in the months to come if the war would allow. Maria handed me a bag with fresh bread and dried fruit in it. She also patted Shakespeare on the head. He loved the attention and grew quite fond of Maria as she was sneaking him slices of bread under the table while the three of us were talking about all we had been through. It seemed they had had quite the experience as well, but seemed much more interested in my experiences of what had happened in town. I told them of the wounded in the churches and some of the kind and not so kind Confederate soldiers I came into contact with. They were also interested by what I observed about some of the citizens in town. They listened to every word I said, but when I mentioned Mr. Burns they rolled their eyes until I mentioned how he went to the Seminary on July 1st and defended the town. Charles looked at me and said, "Really, well maybe we have been wrong about him." Maria joked, "Not so fast, he may be telling everyone about it for years to come whether or not we ask!" All three of us laughed. It was the first time I felt relaxed and it felt good to laugh with my friends the way we did in the good old days.

The time had finally come and sadly it was time to leave. We all went outside and put my supplies in my saddlebags on Chester. We hugged and said our goodbyes and soon we were on our way. As I passed the Christ Lutheran Church, Mary McAllister was talking to a group of people when she spotted me and pointed to Chester. She said, "Is that your missing horse?" I said, "Yes, the good Lord brought him back to me safely." She then looked around a bit frantic asking, "Where is Shakespeare?" When he heard her voice Shakespeare ran to Miss Mary like a flash and jumped up and got her apron dirty. I said, "No, no, Shakespeare, you're getting Miss Mary dirty." Miss Mary waved it off saying, "Oh, my clever little dog, I will miss you," as she patted his head and told me to come back to town soon. I told her that I planned to return in the fall if the war permitted me. I then said goodbye and God Bless and we were on our way home.

As we passed Charles' photography Studio along York Street, the same road we rode in on, I thought back about myself when I entered this town. I was an eager, sometimes brash and arrogant reporter who was looking for that story that would put him on top. This once peaceful town that I came to with the hope of finding some small story to write about has given me more than just a story that I could bury on page ten just to appease my editor as I originally intended. This place has given me an awakening and has turned this brash reporter into a man. To the people who have taught me what it was like to invite a stranger into their town and accept him as one of their own. To the Union soldiers who came to this town to protect us from the approaching enemy and so many who would never return home to their loved ones as I do today. The Confederate soldiers who at first I feared but quickly realized that they were men who had families back home who worried about them the same as Mary my wife worries about me, hoping I stay safe and return home unharmed. The mothers and wives of all these soldiers pray to the very same God in heaven as I do. I thought how very sad this is, we are all brothers and sisters in God's eyes yet we kill one another. I will remember old Mister Burns who was determined that no Confederates will enter his town again if he could help it. And Mrs. Broadhead and little Mary, poor Miss Wade and the very kind Miss McAllister, the brave Miss Salome Myers and all the people of town who opened their hearts and homes to strangers who would fight in this town. Some Union, some Confederate, without questions or excuses, they comforted them all because maybe they saw their fathers and sons who were fighting this war in other parts of the country, maybe just maybe, they hoped if their loved ones were wounded, women of the South would offer this same courtesy. I think the people in town would have done it because it was just the right thing to do; the way God wants us to treat each other. And to the Daughters of Charity who would leave Emmitsburg to travel to Gettysburg to nurse and comfort the bodies and souls of these men, many in the last moments of their lives. Through all of this, I realized I have grown as a person realizing there is more to a story than reporting on an event or war but the people who are involved and the feelings and aspirations they share and friendship they offer. I think I have learned that maybe a story should consist of heart and soul of my fellow man as opposed to the fear and destruction this war has brought. As of Gettysburg...it is a quiet town no more. Forever it will be told of the battle that was fought here and I will do my best to tell my story. I also leave thankful, oh so very thankful to be alive and unharmed as well as to have my fine horse Chester returned to me, instead of taken down south in captivity. And to have found a new little friend in Shakespeare, my little dog, who brought a smile to me as well as a smile and comfort to a few dying soldiers who reminisced about home in their final moments here on earth. "C'mon Shakespeare, let's go to your new home." As I looked up I saw a flock of birds fly by, remembering what that young Confederate soldier told me before he died, of being back home near his fishin' hole as he watched the birds fly by and he sometimes wished he could fly with them. I hope his spirit is with that flock of birds flying back to the place he loved and so badly wanted to return...HOME...I can't think of a more beloved place. May God bless our dear country and as for the town of Gettysburg, thank you and goodbye...

The Town of Gettysburg, Pennsylvania
Courtesy of the Adams County Historical Society

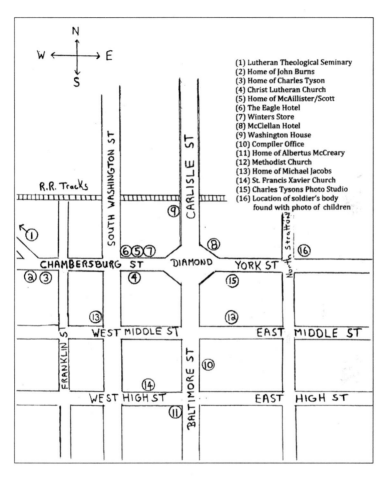

**The map Reporter compiled
after the battle**

CPSIA information can be obtained at www.ICGtesting.com
Printed in the USA
BVOW042020101211

278045BV00001B/2/P